THE LEGACY SERIES

"A brief childhood friendship forms the future of an entire people, neighbors surrender to a coming storm and each other, and a politician risks his life to learn that people, not power, produce the strongest currents. With *Soaked*, Toby LeBlanc gives readers an invigorating collection of stories that provide a fresh reminder of how no one is an island when cataclysmic environmental disasters are certain. Set mostly amid the Louisiana of a not-too distant yet all-too possible future, when living in the aftermath of superstorms means having to reckon with rising water and new technologies, the tales in *Soaked* are an imaginative rendering of what will remain of Louisiana's rich culture and history. LeBlanc plumbs the depths of human nature, questioning whether people can actually change and, if they can, what is lost or saved in the process. A call for people to wake up to the realities of climate change, but to also never forget how to dream, *Soaked* is a collection that sings out its accented regional voice to speak with readers everywhere."

—JOSHUA MYERS
The Indiana Academy

SOAKED

stories

TOBY LeBLANC

CORNERSTONE PRESS
UNIVERSITY OF WISCONSIN-STEVENS POINT

Cornerstone Press, Stevens Point, Wisconsin 54481
Copyright © 2025 Toby LeBlanc
www.uwsp.edu/cornerstone

Printed in the United States of America by
Point Print and Design Studio, Stevens Point, Wisconsin

Library of Congress Control Number: 2024948514
ISBN: 978-1-960329-74-5

Cornerstone Press titles are produced in courses and internships offered by the Department of English at the University of Wisconsin–Stevens Point.

DIRECTOR & PUBLISHER
Dr. Ross K. Tangedal

EXECUTIVE EDITORS
Jeff Snowbarger, Freesia McKee

EDITORIAL DIRECTOR
Brett Hill

SENIOR EDITOR
Ellie Atkinson

PRESS STAFF
Cora Bender, Madalyn Carpenter, Chloe Cieszynski, Mai Kao Hang, Sophie McPherson, Eva Nielsen, Madison Schultz, Ava Willett

For Granny—

I'll bet she's passing a good time up there.

ALSO BY TOBY LeBLANC:

Dark Roux

STORIES

There are flood and drouth
Over the eyes and in the mouth
Dead water and dead sand
Contending for the upper hand.
The parched eviscerate soil
Gapes at the vanity of toil,
Laughs without mirth.
This is the death of the earth.

—T.S. Eliot, "Little Gidding"

The End of the World Bar

He hates the sound of his truck. Ford used to idle different, rev different. You could drive it yourself. This hydrogen model doesn't remind him of gas cars like the online dealer said. And it doesn't even have the anticipating suspension like in the nuclear line. These Louisiana potholes feel more like sinkholes. Many are the beginnings of them.

Don't get Chuck started on the way whiskey tastes now. At least beer is the same. His drone whirs while unpacking cases of brew from the bed of his pickup. The boxy unit rocks on its three-inch wheels as it carries the pallets in its forklift "arms." Several minutes pass while Chuck stares at his roll up interface before he realizes the drone has settled back on its charger, its little robotic forklift arms in lockout position, and the truck is still humming. He taps an icon and his truck rolls away into its normal spot behind the bar before shutting down.

Why would someone open a bar at 8AM? The only sign of life this early is a silent wave from his best friend, the sheriff, as he starts his patrol at Chuck's bar. Boredom is a good answer. His only other pastime (fishing) is a lost cause, seeing as how all the fish are gone. They were taken by other overzealous fishermen, disease, and the brackish, acidic water. Retreating to his empty houseboat in the early morning hours after closing is like lights out on the prison block. Chuck can never sleep until the sun rises. The constant whine of cicadas is likely soothing to younger generations, but without frog chirps to break up their constant scream, it means something always sounds off. Chuck curses the frogs' chytrid extinction at bedtime each night.

Tante Sue used to open her bar even earlier than this. The justification erodes when he considers that Tante Sue was known worldwide and always had a full bar. What he wouldn't give to step back in time when she was alive and he was eighteen, drinking under her neon lights and dancing a Hot-Damn fueled two-step with her at Fred's in Mamou. It would also mean Fred's is not slowly being reclaimed by the marsh, and The End of the World Bar was still landlocked—not at the end of the world.

A chime from the front door severs the memory. Chuck can tell his first customer is a Yankee: his backpack, his hiking shoes (at least he was smart enough to get waterproof ones), and his goofy ball cap. But the dead giveaway is his young face, lineless and optimistic.

"You open?"

"Pretty much."

"Great! Can I get a synthetic latte to go?"

"Syn coffee? Son, this is a bar." Chuck's lips curl at the mention of lab created coffee. While it still provides the buzz everyone has come to expect, and even tastes very similar to the genuine, extinct coffee bean, the process of grinding, brewing, and altering with the sweetener add-ins, is gone. These young ones can't appreciate the process, or even the subtle texture difference, since they never had true, thick Louisiana coffee.

"Oh. K. Thank you." The customer backs away, wondering if the café he was planning to eat at has food.

"Hang on." Chuck disappears into his stock room and fills one of his extra mugs with syn coffee powder and stirs in some hot water. He puts in enough powder to make it like motor oil; somewhat texturally akin to the real coffee his grandmother made. He presents it to the interloper with a practiced smile. The visitor eyes it questioningly.

"No charge unless you want Soy Bailey's in it."

"Y'all do drink a lot down here."

Chuck is pleased to hear a drawl. *So, not a Yankee,* Chuck thinks. It's faint. He used to be able to tell where people were from by their accents, when those existed.

"Where you from?"

"Nashville."

"What made you come here?"

"My mom was from around here. She passed recently. Wanted to see where she grew up."

"I'm sorry to hear that." Chuck means it. He mourned when the local-borns would leave Louisiana for a better life. The Louisiana in them would be bred out, thinned, just like this fellow's accent. But now he is fine with everyone moving away from this soggy, forgotten place as long as they stay alive. "Whereabouts was she born?"

"Baton Rouge."

"No shit. That's been gone for years."

"How long?"

"When Hurricane Pilar came through. She busted the levees."

"Damn. Wish I could have seen it then."

"If you got a few grand, you can go down for a dive tour. I hear there's good spear fishing near the old bank building."

"Oh, I don't dive. This is as close as I get to the water."

"Why's that?"

"Don't trust it."

"Yeah. I know what you mean."

This kid should've seen what life looked like back in Venice, before Katrina. Sure, Chuck was only three. But he can remember watching the boats come in. Shrimp, crab, snapper, redfish, specs…they flowed from the water, through the town, and into his father's bar at the dead end of the peninsula everyone called "The End of the World." When Katrina took out the town, his Cajun momma moved them back home where she knew hurricanes could be managed. His father's broken heart almost changed the name of his new bar. But the ever-fishing Cajuns recognized the brand too easily. Economics won over broken hearts. It didn't used to be like that either.

The front door chimes again. Rosco arrives before his appointed time. He knows how lonely Chuck must be to open this early. Mostly because he's the same amount of lonely.

"Rosco! You trying to face the day? Or be done with it?"

"Gimme something that'll fix both," Rosco declares shaking off his coat.

"Whiskey it is."

Rosco eyes the stranger suspiciously before looking at his full coffee mug with even more distrust.

"Stick to the whiskey, kid. I'll buy. There's a reason they call it syn coffee. It's a sin to drink it."

"Oh. Thank you. But …" The visitor is stopped by Rosco's look. Replacing his words is a nod to acknowledge feeling both welcome and threatened. They toast and shoot before Rosco orders beers for the house.

"Man, I'm ready for this rain to stop." Rosco rehashes the rehearsed conversation he always has with Chuck in the mornings.

"I hear you," Chuck replies.

The visitor, fuzzy with early booze burn, half scoffs. "But doesn't it rain non-stop here?"

Both natives look at him incredulously. He doesn't know how this works. The safety of monotony is what cuts through the uncertainty of hurricanes, droughts, floods, or if the Amazon drones will fight the storms to deliver to this water-logged outpost on time. Chuck's face softens. Before Rosco can dress down the poor boy any further, Chuck interjects: "We have a saying. If you act like it'll never stop, it won't."

Rosco de-bristles. "My tomatoes are saturated. I'm going to lose them all if it doesn't let up at least a little."

"Y'all have enough sun for those?" the kid chimes in again. Rosco eyes him a little more closely.

"Where you from? Shreveport? Dallas?" Rosco interrogates.

"Nashville." Chuck responds, turning up the bar lights from his interface.

"You're a tourist in Lafayette?" Rosco asks with marked disbelief.

"His momma was from Baton Rouge," Chuck responds, trying to temper him.

"What kind of industry do you have here?"

Rosco blinks at the question and turns to Chuck to see if the nomad is serious. Chuck's response is a smile and a shrug.

"Why? Are you looking to invest? 'Cause I got some projects I need to get off of the ground."

"Yeah? What kind of work do you do?"

Rosco smiles again at Chuck. "Why, I'm an engineer."

"Really? What kind?"

"He's messing with you. He's a Levee Technician."

"Oh." The meddler's tone is one of polite, impressed confusion.

"His job is to walk levees. Look for breaches. Fix breaches."

"River levees?"

"All levees. River, farming, gulf…"

"Gulf? You all built levees for the gulf?"

Both seventy-year-olds gawk at the young one. Tasting the tension amidst the wet air, Chuck doesn't want to lose half of his morning business. "What kind of work do you do, friend?"

"Me?" the trespasser says sheepishly. "I do some coding. Mostly logistics programs. I do some art, too. Don't like being too tied down to anything."

"He's an artist, Chuck."

"Calm down, Rosco. You're just mad he can pull more ass than you. Tell him about how the girls line up, friend."

The last line causes the visitor to meet their eyes, one by one. He nervously busies himself with his watch interface, seeming to respond to something.

"Thank you for the drinks. It's time for me to go."

"Whoa. What got said?" Rosco attempts.

"It's just time for me to go."

"The artist thing?"

"Shit. No," Chuck interjects with recognition. "He's not interested in *girls* lining up. Man, I'm sorry. I'm…shit."

"Have a good day."

"Let us make it up to you."

The new guy smiles and exits. The chime rings pleasantly. The two men watch the door in silence.

"Damn."

"Don't worry about it, Chuck."

"I'm worried about it and everything that could happen because of it." He hunches his shoulders while he cleans the visitor's mug. When he was young it was called heterocentrism. Now it's just homophobic.

"Like what?"

"Like a bad review."

"People don't read those. The worse that'll happen is old Adeleide from across the street spied our friend walking out of here and makes a gossip tabloid readout thing."

Chuck brings his eyes up to Rosco while the old artifact drains the last of his beer. "Reddit," he corrects uselessly. Rosco's aversion to tech and anything digitally social goes all the way back to his twenties, to the point music apps are still new-fangled to him. This translated into Rosco being one of the last holdouts in the oil extraction division of a big three company before they transitioned to reclaiming plastic and renewable energy. It's not worth arguing with him. The mud and concrete under a levee tech's rubber boots won't choke off more of his business if he's a homophobe. Rosco and the levees are made for each other. Constructed of men and the earth, they each try to keep back the inevitable. Their strength lies only in their simplicity. Simplicity demands they never change. Even when everything on the planet (including the planet itself) has changed, the people here never will. The mud walker slides the empty mug to Chuck, beer foam still stuck to the stubble on his lip.

"One more before I have to go to work. Please."

Chuck pours and walks back to his stock room to replace his freshly washed coffee mug. The slump in his shoulders deepens as he passes the digital projection of the previous bar, the first incarnation of The End of the World in Venice. His body feels the image without needing to glance at it on his desk. The picture, taken from outside the bar's whitewashed walls, documents his family's legacy: two bars undone by water. The second is meeting a slow, and much less violent death. This city is now caressed by the Gulf courtesy of a large chunk of the Antarctic glacier breaking off two summers before, raising the sea level ten feet higher than at the turn of the century. The economic erosion is all but complete already. That, combined with a sinking state and a hundred-mile-wide scar cut from the coast to Lafayette by Hurricane Pilar fifty years earlier, solidified the fate of this state: Louisiana will wash away. This part of the region, from the middle of the foot of Louisiana's boot, to the coast, had always been a geologic ephemeral dream. The land here was past the continental shelf, only borrowed from the ocean. As Chuck slowly makes his way back to his solitary customer, the view of the old bar pulls at him. Its sparsely-shingled, low-slung roof and glass block windows were home to him once. He thinks about his options and what it felt like for his parents to walk away from that bar. This bar always asks him to stay a little longer. He'd always regret leaving. Returning to his post at the bar, he finds Rosco knocking a beat out alongside Warren Storm, who sings through the micro speakers embedded in the walls. Chuck smiles since this nanotech expenditure can be appreciated by the biggest luddites.

"You finally figured out how to connect to the jukebox app!" Chuck applauds daintily.

"Daughter was in town this past weekend. Just remembered she showed me. They don't make music like this anymore!" Rosco says, beginning to bop his head like a hip-hop artist.

"It's from a better time."

"Can you imagine what it must have been like?"

"What?"

"I mean back then. Things were all beginning. The economy. You know."

"Yeah."

"I think a lot about what it was like during my grandad's time. When oil was king."

Chuck clears his throat. He clears it again, trying to get the argument to dislodge and slither down his gullet. It's pointless, he knows. But if he acts like it will never stop, it never will. Like everything else in this place, he's saturated.

"You and I both know what happened there."

"Yeah!" Rosco says in time with music. "They started making electric cars and using biodegradable shit."

"It started before that, Rosco. Venice and Buras got wiped out when I was just four. It was the MRGO that brought it there. And to New Orleans."

"New Orleans was dead weight. Full of 'artists' like your friend that just left." Rosco made sure to gesture giant sarcastic quotation marks around "artist."

Chuck goes to his phone and hits "STOP" on his jukebox app. "Last call, Rosco."

"Not you, too. You as sensitive as that Yank?" The s's in "sensitive" drag.

"You're prattling on about people who leveled two of my homes!"

"Look, you old buzzard. I obviously don't want any water in anybody's house. I'm a Levee Tech for crissakes. My whole life is dedicated to keep us dry. Don't act like you wouldn't mind some of that cash our parents and grandparents made." Rosco slams back his beer and pulls his hood over his balding head right before laying his thumb over the Bitcoin register to pay for his tab. "It's time for me to take my watch." The door politely chimes as he exits into the drizzle and grey.

Chuck cleans Rosco's glass in jagged silence. He stares out into the hardening rain. His hopes that Rosco comes back tomorrow, punctuated by how he hates his guts, creates suction in his brain. Memories are sediment lying at the bottom of his murky mind. Disturb them and they will only become blinding. The once-living rot releases its guts and sucks anything with the possibility of creating life and liveliness into a dead zone. He has to get out of this bar, this place. The rest of the world can't be drowning like this. He thinks of visiting his sister in the mountains. She was able to say goodbye years ago. Memories don't rot for her. They run downriver, or in her case, upriver. She's so happy where she is. He's sure all the weed she smokes must help.

That could be all he needs: a little change. He could start selling pot. There's only one dispensary in town, and it only does pot. What if he did syn coffee, too? People wouldn't need to go anywhere else. What is he talking about? He'd have to learn all kinds of new laws and policies. Weed has more variety than alcohol. And forget working those space aged syn coffee mixers. But if he had a full bar from morning to night, he'd hire someone. Maybe even a few people.

This is where the dream stops. There aren't enough people here to even do the jobs available. The odds of him getting another grizzled old holdout like himself, probably giving up higher pay, are low. The odds of him finding some kid looking for a buck are lower. Let's face it, this was the last state to change the drinking age to twenty-one and the last state to go carbon neutral. Louisiana will wash away before it changes. *What used to be our way of living, of holding on to our identity, is what's drowning us,* Chuck thinks.

"Enough," he says aloud. "Juke… play Pop Classics."

If he acts like this can't stop, it never will. He can't beat back the oppressive chaos he lives in. Trying to eke out this banal life to feel stable in the constantly shifting world certainly doesn't feel like living either. *If you can't beat the chaos, join it,* he thinks. There's only one thing left—throw a party. For a third of a millennium, this part of the world had learned to make a dead end the party everyone wanted to come to. If the dead end moves not once, but twice, shouldn't that make it twice the party? Moving with the world is what survival is now. Being a bartender in this outpost is sacred. He won't let it all wash away.

Returning to the back room, he forces his feet to walk in time with classic Taylor Swift songs. He finds his holiday decorations and rips them from their mold resistant plastic coating. He whistles along with Big Freedia as he decks the halls. He runs out lights and artificial garland around his sign outside just like he does every September. He finishes with a Santa Claus hat atop his head. He puts several Mardi Gras masks on tabletops but saves one for his face. He makes sure to separate the biodegradable Jack-o'-Lanterns from the old plastic ones. Only the plastic ones will hold up outside. He slips his arms into the Monk robe he wore while tending bar last Halloween. He pulls out every vegan sausage he'd bought for the week's happy hour and lights his electric pit. Somehow, he'd managed to keep the leftover fireworks dry. Opening a window, he tosses lit bottle rockets out into the street.

"Juke… Shuffle Holiday Mix."

Monster Mash, Professor Longhair, and Donald Glover's remake of that Faith Hill Christmas song scream alongside the bottle rockets. And Chuck screams alongside both. Each shriek and howl that Chuck releases dries the dampness from around him. His body moves to the beat as if is seeing an old friend after too long a parting. The gyrating and twerking stir the sediment of memories within him. A full bar, full of life, full of forgetting, populates his clearing mind. Another bar being born—this bar—complete with ribbon cutting by the mayor, bubbles up in his brain. The memory has all the past, complete with an indomitable will to surge forward inherited from his parents, as well as hope for the future: a new frontier for The End of the World.

The bass shakes Chuck's walls, breaking his agreement with the business across the street. Adeleide Ryan, of Adeleide's Recycled Clothes, made Chuck promise he'd never do this before 1PM. As he lets another rocket hiss through the window, he understands this will upend the delicate peace of this town. But that's why he does it. Adeleide needs some life. Specifically, she needs some living that can't be gossiped about, only told, like a story in a bar. Chuck knows she's hunkered down with her hand to her phone implant by her ear, calling 911. It doesn't matter that the last mass shooting was twenty-two years ago. Between the broken rules, the smoke, explosions, and some stranger leaving the bar just prior to this nonsense, Chuck's sure she's got his best friend, the sheriff, on the line and she is trying to convince the peace officer that Chuck's one-man party is the apocalypse. *The slumber this town has sunk into is the apocalypse*, Chuck thinks.

In less than a minute, his suspicions are proven true. The sheriff exits his patrol vehicle tentatively. The lawman makes a bullet-stop for the curious crowd forming behind him with Adeleide right behind the sheriff. It looks as if he is leading them toward the uncommon din inside and around the bar, like a piper using danger to lure citizens from lives as dull as the weather. It would take a while for the fire department to arrive since it has to come all the way from Pineville. Inundation means fire departments aren't typically needed and the governor pruned "unneeded resources" from the state like dead blossoms on a camelia. Without back up from the hose boys, the sheriff looks alone, even in front of the crowd. This sheriff has not encountered violence, except for the occasional fist fight in this bar, in roughly twenty years. The officer's hand shakes over his gun, a weapon likely never used in the line of duty.

Remembering has always been a favorite pastime in this part of the world. Even when things are better than in the past, people of Louisiana look backward more than forward. Chuck reconsiders his opinion on remembering. Maybe nostalgia is not all poison in the veins. Maybe a jolt of certain memories would do everyone some good. The world is wild. And the people in this place come from wild stock. He remembers when they weren't scared or bored. His best friend didn't look so nervous investigating loud noises from party favors. Maybe if they remember how life can move and flow like the water around them, they can face the world as it is.

Through the haze of gunpowder smoke, Chuck surveys the confused faces of the crowd. Chuck can see sparks of curiosity, wonderment, excitement, and, in a few, relief. It makes them look younger; flecks of what was make Chuck believe it can all come back. The water didn't wash it all away. Their wildness is just damp. Dry it off, light it, and they can explode to life again. Chuck gambles that the line between his giddiness and their fear is thin enough to push them over, back into living out loud like their ancestors did in this part of the world. He doesn't have a plan for how to bring this out of them. This place never goes as planned anyway. For only a moment, he considers what he is doing, what it looks like, and what could be at stake. It serves only to steel his nerve. He just hopes this crazed grip on rejoicing rubs off on them.

As the sheriff leads the soggy mob inside, Chuck lights the handful of firecrackers in his hand, hoping the chaos is enough to remind them where they live and what they are made of. Chuck drops the band of firecrackers over the bar and dives to the floor. As they pop, Chuck's bestie fires into the smoke, his shaking hands making bullets rain into and around the bar.

From behind the bar, on his belly, Chuck coughs through blue smoke. He hears gasps and screams. Their fear is only a fever-pitch from happiness. He will remind them how to be unflinching as the world drowns. He laughs out his announcement: "Welcome back to the End of the World Bar! Everyone drinks free today!"

Relief

Aging has not been what Arlis thought it would be. He gets up in the morning with tons of energy, but it is gone by noon. He can remember numbers and names as long as you don't talk while he's reciting them to himself. But he's gotten more optimistic rather than falling into a stereotypical later-life grump. None would believe it, though, the way his face remains flat and expressionless at nearly all times.

His body tells the story clearly. His doctor calls his newest issue "vertigo." After months of procrastination, the only reason he made an appointment at the federal clinic is because the vertigo interfered with his mission. The doctor was nice, and he might have trusted her, but he will never trust the nanotech treatment she suggests. A career working for the Fed taught him nothing they purported to "help" did any such thing. Captain Miller of the Cajun Navy says the vertigo is just a natural side effect of being married to the water. Arlis's body will stay lonesome for water when he's away. Despite Captain Miller's authority coming from an unofficial, private, volunteer, socially-focused entity, Arlis appreciated some explanation. It makes sense to him that his old job in the Coast Guard feigning control over the unpredictable left him impotent in many ways. Forty plus years of riding the waves, weathering the storms, pulling bodies from the wet grave, and pointing a fully automatic weapon, aches in his weary knees and lower back.

He rathers that explanation than consider his belly growing (from all the thank you dishes he gets from his new job) could be putting undue strain on his joints. He doesn't need a doctor or the Fed to assess the wear on his body, held together with loosening sallow skin, to tell him he's gotten fat.

Everyone at the landing gives him a wide berth, mainly because of the dissonance between his lack of expression and his pleasant disposition. He seems too happy to be working among the exhausted holdouts inhabiting these islands beyond the levees. This is the most life Arlis has ever seen. The mangrove water is friendly. Or, rather, the salt grass, houses, and levees are friendly; collections of humanity amidst the water. These folks risk everything to continue calling South Louisiana home. Despite flood insurance ceasing to exist after Hurricane Pilar, only people like this can live here, mainly because they don't know how to exist anywhere else. The tepid saltwater sloshes lazily over the hybrid outboard engine on his Rigid Hull Inflatable Boat. The motion of the craft is gentle and responsive, things his former Coast Guard boat could never be. It's a perfect venue for the mission he has retired into: relief.

First stop is Mr. Hebert. The elderly man has more hair than Arlis. His posture in his wheelchair is better and his waistline is smaller. Last week, Mr. Hebert texted that his porch was collapsing. Every foot of living space counts when his entire world hangs precariously on carbon fiber, cement-filled pillars. It's not like the ninety-three-year-old can get his wheelchair up and down the twenty feet of stairs to the small dry patch of dirt below. An exosuit would solve the problem, but Mr. Hebert, like many of the sodden residents of these marshy islands, doesn't trust technology lo-jacked into his brain. So many of the older generation don't like the metal and plastic of these suits even if they allow the wearer to move in ways not possible in years. Stepping into these prosthetic sheaths create artificial barriers with the world when the people wearing them already feel too removed from the life they should be living, something Arlis completely understands. Exosuits are too expensive anyway. Mr. Hebert even gave up on his automated lift this year. Salt air corrodes any metal in the custom-made elevator Arlis's organization fabricated for him, making it seize up regularly. Mr. Hebert once got stuck for four hours in mid-descent to a boat below.

The land his house perches on is special, being neither marsh nor one of the long chenier ridges that oak trees still manage to grow on. It's an old high point of this parish, leftover land haunting the water. Mr. Hebert watches Arlis laboriously climb the two flights, eyes peering from his front door, giving his home the appearance of an obese but watchful heron standing amidst the four-foot-tall oyster grass, face in the wind, waiting for word from the gulf of fate.

The dilapidated porch is a tangible piece of better times when Mr. Hebert's wife was alive, before the house was raised as the land sunk and the ocean came to find them. Arlis will often listen to stories about their life well after the sun is below the horizon and the wind turns the tops of the salt grass back toward the sea. The images of their love sparkle behind Mr. Hebert's cataracts. The collection of dark splotches on his cheeks, gathered like storm clouds from stubborn refusal of sunscreen, become slightly lighter and less ominous. Mostly it's Mr. Hebert telling his same stories, making his same comments:

"Poo yie but dis rain!"

"Back in '25, Pilar came and washed away so much…"

"My wife, she was da best cook. She could make a dark gumbo, fry up fish…"

Being in the proximity of that kind of love soothes an ache Arlis has never been able to name. That's why this Cajun Navy thing has been so nice. It feels good. It's people helping people, instead of helping the Fed help itself to whatever it can dry off. In lieu of tending a coast no one can really map anymore, much less guard, Arlis brings boards to a grieving old man, mail to those the Amazon drones' GPS can't find because addresses shift with the tides, and food to those who can't get to a market. He must remind himself constantly there isn't a document to fingerprint verify. Human interaction is valued over productivity in this gig. It's worth more than his time, and it feels more fulfilling than his pension. When his watch beeps with a message or dispatch, it doesn't have to be cleared through a commanding officer. The only command is to provide help in whatever form it should take. In this case, it's just a conversation with a lonely old man.

He leaves the composite planks in the space beneath the house. Other spryer members of the Cajun Navy, likely wearing the strength and motion enhancing exosuits the old timer doesn't trust, will arrive to do young men's work. As he pulls away from Mr. Hebert's house, having shared a cup of synthetic coffee and some nostalgia, he realizes it only took his whole career to end up in the Navy he'd thought he'd signed up for.

Only a half mile or so from the soon to be renewed Hebert house, he wonders why he left. There are no more planned stops today. The channels on his cell watch are quiet. His home behind the levee wall won't do. It's not part of his mission. At home he gives no relief, and he finds none either. While the quiet of this domesticated water is soothing, the quiet at home is painful. There lives a void left by his first wife, the sea. It drives him to inventory the contents of his fridge on his roll-up interface most nights while languishing on his couch, debating which leftovers he should add to the anchor weight growing over his belt. Food gives him the temporary experience of tenderness. Much more of these homecooked thank you's and his thick masts of legs will struggle against the wages of inactivity. His waistline is not the worst casualty, though. The bit below his waist could be all but forgotten. During deployments he didn't have to worry about it. But he'd remember just how bad his case of the flops was when he'd arrive at shore. Eventually he couldn't get it up at all. As age found him, and the bitterness between him and salty water grew, he stopped caring. He's hoping someone here can revive him if that's not too much to ask.

As he daydreams of a faceless woman and the touch she'd give without asking him to pay, he nearly misses a strange grove of trees. Passing through patches of black mangroves, he happens upon foliage which shouldn't be on this side of the levee wall; close to where Gueydan used to be. It's not uncommon for the remaining land to shift in this region. But this island harbors azaleas and honeysuckle clambering across thriving cypress. Typically, cypress left here in this salt are skeletons, last alive when he left for the Coast Guard in '31. More worrisome is a small tunnel through the foliage, possibly leading to some sort of cove; a perfect hiding place for pirates. Thieves and other ne'er-do-wells stage their goods in these types of places and move before anyone can find them. Poachers, too, will find whatever animal research traps are placed here and plunder them. These need to be inspected by hand since GPS and satellite are no good for land constantly on the move. He begrudgingly sends up his small drone and it hums into position over the island. The camera can see nothing through the dense canopy. Irritated gusts of sea breeze make it hard to guide the drone back, and the chop of the water makes it even harder to land. The wind hushes momentarily, just long enough for him to feel dank humidity crawl up his spine and make every crevice feel like a sauna. This weather has never rendered aid to him.

He will have to inspect the cove himself. A thought of calling in for assistance is quickly chased away. His job is to help, not to be helped. It feels good to follow an instinct other than how long to microwave his meals. But he checks himself. He's spent years "helping" the Fed, but all he did was protect their economic interests. Part of why he left was because he he'd finally acquired some wisdom and could tell the difference between helping and protecting. Today, whether he tracks newly broken off vegetation, or confiscates and returns stolen property, he just wants to help.

He idles slowly, looking for signs of underwater debris. The last thing he needs is his prop hung up in old nylon lines or to have this tactical vessel instantly deflated by silt-covered edges of sunken trash. This close to shore, with all the runoff of North America filtering through these border islands, it's impossible to tell what's in the water until you are on top of it. Advanced depth finding and satellite imagery can't protect anyone here from the trash of previous generations. He ducks low as he approaches the opening in the brush.

Birds cover the impossible island: egrets, seagulls, and even a couple of pelicans. Blackberries the size of corks dangle from their woven briars. He has just enough room to make it through with his boat. Thorns hiss as they scrape across the nylon covering the gunwales. When he spots an opening in the briar, he lets out the breath he'd only just realized he was holding. Huffing at the realization he's spooked, he yanks a blackberry and tastes it. It's sweeter than his childhood memories can recall. The flora tunnel has led him to a calm, sweet smelling pond. It's a welcome ten degrees cooler in here, making him relax somewhat. There are no signs of illicit activity that he can see. The water of the pond has the appearance of blackened glass, likely from the overlay of the dense tree canopy. It's a few moments before his eyes adjust from the grey light outside the cove to the dimness inside. He cuts the motor and notices how loud the electric hum of the idle was. Fragrance intensifies and color jumps at him to mock the dimness filtered through canopy. Because he stares at the ceiling of leaves above, remembering what it was like to lay in a grove of trees, he doesn't see his boat drifting toward the edge of the mirrored pond.

The first sound he recognizes as the sound of his hollow inflated boat bumping against something. But the second sound is felt more than heard. His guard raises as he understands this place is more than it seems. He stares at the tree, wondering if this is all a fake menagerie; some silk and plastic construction made by an artist with a sense of humor like the guy who put a Prada store in the middle of the desert of Marfa, Texas. That would at least make sense of the species in this place. He runs his fingers over the trunk, the leaves, and the water. Bark flakes off the pine. The needles poke at his skin. When he tastes the water he is sure it is real, though he thinks it might be fresh. He leans closer to tree and its roots. He sees something white, orange, and blue beneath the undergrowth.

A new, sharp sound, slices through his curiosity and demands respect. The pump action of a shotgun is unmistakable. Arlis is pissed more than he is scared. There were no signs of people when he entered the cove, but he hadn't done a thorough search. That's a rookie move. His gun is behind him. In a former life he would easily turn, grab, drop, aim, and shoot. With this belly, though, the turning itself will take all that time. Even if he could, his vertigo would likely disorient him. He raises his hands instead.

"Drop the gun in the water."

Focus is momentarily deterred by a woman's voice. He's heard of many women in the pirating business, using the old gender roles to get clueless residents to cough up valuables. Arlis returns to debating his odds. If she has the drop on him and is not ready to take the shot, or she's a bad shot, he still could aim his gun. If the odds are anything like his instincts today, though, that wouldn't end well. Why end life here when it is supposed to be beginning again, anyway? He slowly reaches down for his retirement present: a federal issue, recoil neutralizing, history-deleted assault rifle, and dips it into the pool. It disappears into the black unceremoniously without a sound.

"Leave this place."

He searches his memory for a recollection of this voice. It's definitely not the voice of any woman he's helped in the Acadia Parish area. He's marked voices of would-be mates for after he gets this little dangle problem taken care of. She's not from here and likely doesn't know his job is just to help. She's probably been robbed a few times, hence the shotgun. The novelty of her accent, or maybe the unwavering resoluteness, forces his neck to turn.

"You're getting real close to both kinds of holy."

Stopping, he thinks about the joke in her threat, and sniffs out a laugh. She likely misses his appreciation of her humor due to his lack of expression. Nothing follows. She isn't going to shoot, he decides. Nobody threatens twice. He needs to see who this is. He turns.

Water explodes next to him. The shot echoes five times across the mill pond. He ducks into the boat, realizing the instinct spurning him to this action didn't assess for his rubber gunwales and how they do nothing for gunfire. Wetness gushing over his shoulder tells him he may not have to convince her of this fact. He finds the source of the gushing and sees water instead of blood. Relief of being uninjured is fleeting. The shotgun blast has the pond spewing through a large hole in the side of his boat. She's still out there. It's better to lay still, let her think she killed him, and go down with the boat. He can still hold his breath for three minutes. When she loses interest, he can come back up and sneak behind her somehow.

Beneath the black, glassy surface he sees the water is in fact very clear. Normally, he'd have to be sixty miles out before there could be this little silt and debris, the pieces of Louisiana drifting away into the deep. He slows his movements, blowing out some of his air to sink a bit, as he was trained to do. In his heyday he could hold his breath for five and a half minutes. He won't need that long today. He measures time by the ache of his lungs and looks around. To his left are the roots of the pine he'd bumped into along with white, orange, and blue things he spied earlier. The water clarity allows him to see nothing but things: bottles, jugs, tarps, tanks, and even old life jackets combining to make a giant, floating island. How any of these plants could flourish on plastic is inconceivable. A glance below shows him the bottom is matted debris as well. His gun is there, but it's too far down to get on this breath. Whether he goes for it or not, he must surface. He ventures a look back upward to see the sky only slightly darkened by the tint of this water. Clear vision upward means he must be visible as well. He waits a little longer for his lungs to shout and then kicks upward.

The water breaks gently, and Arlis breathes as evenly as his stretched chest will allow. He looks for the source of the voice. His eyes land on a cottage, or maybe a shack, he had not seen when he putted in. He knows he looked in that direction, though. It's like it appeared. The burn of inadequacy from making so many careless mistakes mixes with the acid already building in his legs from treading water. It leads him to make another oversight.

"You were real committed to playing possum," the woman's voice says from the place it has moved to, behind him once again.

"Yes ma'am."

"It's 'yes ma'am' now. You always so nice to people whose property you trespassing on?"

Her accent leaves her words severed at times, softly plodding by at others. He knows it, forgetting where from. "Especially the ones who have a gun to my back. Can you tell me what this place is? Who you are?"

"Is this something you own?"

"What?"

"Do you own this place? Do you own me?"

"No ma'am."

"Then why do you think you can ask questions?"

"I'm part of the Cajun Navy. Didn't recognize this place and thought I would check it out."

"So, you *did* think you owned this place. And wanting to help gave you the deed. Now you need help. Who has your deed?"

Arlis's arms are tired. He hasn't tread water like this in years. And he's sure this water is all fresh since he's not buoyed like normal. He doesn't know where this is going, but he is completely out of choices.

"You do."

"Only for now." The safety clicks. "Swim over to the house."

As he freestyles to the plastic shore, he thinks about how this is all wrong. He'd come into this place trying to help his neighborhood. For his trouble, his life is in danger. He places his hands on roots intertwined with plastic. His white wicking tee plasters to his big belly. All of this is out of place, not him. He considers turning to look at his captor, but last time he was so bold she'd put a hole in the side of his boat. Come to think of it, he had nary a piece of shot in his skin. Seems impossible she'd fire a scatter gun at him and only hit the intended target. Or, had she hit her target? His feet echo through the underbrush of hollow plastic. The barrel presses against his back, and he pushes open the door to the shack.

Inside the air is warm bread, it's blankets and well-preserved memory. Breathing it is remembering. It's lit only with naked low wattage LED bulbs, but the light seems to bleed into every corner. There exists not an inch of wall space absent of crucifixes or portraits of the Virgin Mary. Each looks as if it has come from a different culture, maybe a different country. But despite changes in skin color or different shaped noses, the eyes are unmistakably the same. All bear weary compassion in their gaze. The woman moves from behind

Arlis, grabbing something to his left. Still remaining out of sight, she holds a towel out in front of him.

"Sit. I'll get you syn coffee." The sudden change in protocol makes his feet glue to the floor. This could be a trap. "You're a terrible listener. I tell you to leave and you stay. I tell you to sit and you stand. No wonder you need so much help. I'll be nice and I'll ask. Please would you sit?"

Arlis keeps his hands raised slightly above his waist so she can trust he will do as she says. The oak chair screeches across a cypress wood floor. It's all in good condition. Seems strange none of this is rotted, sitting only inches above water that he knows must splash during the big storms. Stranger still is the coolness of it all. He hears no hums or growls of generators.

"How do you take it?"

"What?"

"The syn coffee. How do you take it?"

"Black with a teaspoon of sugar."

"Figures."

"What?"

She says nothing else while pouring. Finally, before him, he is able to see her. She could be his age, but he's not sure. The lines around her eyes and mouth hint at the passage of years. Her body is lithe. The inactivity of surviving on islands in isolation hasn't plagued her. Her eyes aren't dulled from the monotony of waves on the horizon. They are sharp and dark, nearly black. Her hair is interwoven with many colors: black here, gray there, and seasoned with cayenne and amber. Her nose is rounded with a slight downward curl, the latter something left over from a French grandparent, he guesses. But her skin is not French. Her arms don't have brown patches or liver spots like his does. When he allows his eyes to come up to hers, she is peering through him.

"Satisfied?" She waits for him to answer. He is embarrassed. Across from him she sips loudly, enjoying the black liquid as if there were still coffee plants producing in South America or Africa. Her bored gaze ventures out of the open door they'd entered the room through, lost in some pleasant thought. Edges of her mouth bend in amusement. It leaves Arlis questioning if all her company arrives at gunpoint. "Well?"

It had not occurred to him that she still expected an answer. He would have used the same question to show a new enlistment how stupid they were to try something their way. In boot camp, he would intentionally ask questions to make recruits wonder if they knew their asshole from their earhole. Arlis can see now how he'd missed her tone, just like everything else in this place.

"Yes."

She lets out one hard note, a laugh of disbelief, before pointing her black eyes, infinitely more intimidating than her shotgun, at him.

"You're like your coffee. You think a small, sweet lie can cover up a lot of bitter truth. Why'd you come here?"

"Ma'am—"

"It's Sarah."

"Ms. Sarah, I was passing by, just got done helping Mr. Hebert—Do you know Mr. Hebert?" Despite her pleasant smile, her black hole eyes continue to bore. "Anyway, like I said, I saw this place, didn't recognize it. I thought I would have a look in case anyone needed anything."

"You mean in case you needed anything. No one here asked you for help. You were curious, and you wanted to feel strong again. This is a place your memory and your technology don't own. That must have been intolerable. Because here you are, nearly forcing your way here. You would have come in this place telling me what I need, I'm sure, had the Virgin not let me know you were on the little pond. You'd say I need to get out of this place. I need to rejoin society." Arlis gulps his syn coffee. Looking into the cup he sees the same blackness of the pond, the shotgun, and her eyes. "Isn't that right?"

The accent finally makes sense. This woman is Creole. Trying to place her accent and her blended heritage distract him from assessing the method and intent of her questions. Her questions don't fit the hostage training that was re-administered every five years in the Coast Guard. His seniority allowed him to skip the last two. He tries to convince himself a decade was not enough time to forget everything. Captors had specific things they wanted to know, or at least categories for them to fall into. It was a process he trusted; a process he knew had a definite outcome. Knowing her motive would make this a whole lot simpler and him a whole lot calmer. He noticed she didn't like his questions. She tolerated statements, especially answers. She'll likely remind him again who is in charge if he tries another question.

"There's a lot of plastic underneath us."

"What's left of an old recycling plant."

"How did—"

She pulls a kitchen knife from underneath the table. It's thin and razor sharp. The edge has been filed back from generations of honing. The glint of pure silver defies the humidity that attacks it, maybe even by cutting through it. That knife should be rusted through out here. Her black eyes, sharper than the knife, level on him.

"I want love," Arlis says with nearly childlike resignation. Fear and sadness converge on his face. The confusion, the intimidation, the way she looks at him greased the truth he'd thought he buried, even from himself. His air catches in his lungs as the words hang between them. She grabs a pear from the bowl on the table and starts to cut it. Where is she getting pears? Seconds lumber by while he waits for her to laugh again, or maybe stab him. A perfect slice of fruit enters her mouth. Her lips purse with each bite. She watches him again. Her look is both bored and expectant. "I– I don't know how to get it."

It's like when he was eight, telling his father he didn't know how to launch a boat. Only Sarah's eyes hold none of his father's disappointment. Piece by piece the pear enters her mouth. This is silly. There's never been a need to think about love, much less talk about it. Arlis's little outburst couldn't be what her interrogation is aimed at, despite how content she seems to be with his discomfort. She's looking for something else. He doesn't want to stick around to find out what it is.

"Ma'am, can I go now?"

"You think love belongs to you?"

"Ma'am?"

"You think love's something to make your own. Like you thought about my home." She slips another slice of pear into her mouth, chewing slowly and thoughtfully. "You can leave at any time. But how are you going to do that with your boat at the bottom of the pond?" The black glass in her eyes soften and a smile lights her face. "You're one hell of a last patient. What's your name?"

"Arlis."

"Arlis I'm a *traiteuse*. A faith healer. The last one, I'd guess. I'd given it up. It's been three years since I treated. I was done. But last night Jesus and the Virgin visited me. They told me I had one patient left, and he would be here today."

"You knew I'd be here? Then why did you shoot at me?"

"Jesus said I would know you by your *tête dur*, your hard head. The gun seemed the surest way to figure out how stubborn you are. I don't want you here. But Jesus and Mary apparently do."

Arlis debates again if she really is that good of a shot. Putting that next to her method of interrogation elicits respect from him. Whether it be auditory hallucinations, or Jesus Himself, Arlis loosens with her lack of intent kill him. She's softening, too. He can tell. He gambles one last time with a question mixed with humor.

"Faith-healer? You heal people's faith?"

Sarah smiles even wider. Having lost the threat of death, Arlis can now admit she is beautiful. She lets out her single syllable laugh. "Yeah. That happens, too. But mostly I heal bodies."

Ambiguity and non sequiturs led them to talking about bodies. The burn of inadequacy he'd felt out in the pond engulfs his chest and moves outward toward his extremities. The career he'd left taught him to ignore his body and push past its false limits of pain and fatigue. He isn't ready to open up about his physical health to a lady floating on a trash island and suffering from a mental health issue. It scares him how he's already said too much. Never has he felt like he could completely connect with people. It doesn't matter if she's beautiful or if her questions are genuine. The comfort sneaking up on him is not trustworthy. Oscillating poles, conversation and silence, comfort and violence, shake the foundation he's built for himself, leaving his knees hurting and his head swimming. He rises from his chair, and the dark wells of her eyes follow him. Her jaw continues to work on the pear, never breaking its rhythm. Watching its motion reminds him of the sea and his vertigo returns. His hands smack the table as he steadies himself. The bottom of his belly pressing against the top of the table helps. He's not leaving, not anytime soon. It's not because of the sunken boat either. It's not because of a long swim to an empty house with an unbelievable story. Land sickness is only an excuse. His body's response confirms he can't leave, because he'd be walking away from the most interest anyone has ever shown him.

"I can't get hard."

His ears hear it before he realizes it's him that said it. The "d" echoes around the tiny impossible shack the same way her gunshot echoed around the pond. The vertigo intensifies and sends him to his chair. It disappears when his butt is back in the seat, as if this could be the only place the world is not trying to wash out from underneath him. Replacing the shifting in his head is the lava of inadequacy bubbling up through his chest and face. The reality of his tired pecker out where the world can know it leaves him unsure of how he'll continue living with this soul-splitting honesty in the air.

"Or maybe you been hard for too long, and God decided he'd teach you how to be soft, starting at your body." He assumes this means something to her since she is looking at him as if it should mean something. He is supposed to be hard. That was his job, after all. He stood hard against the storms, hard against the intruders of the country, and hard against the orders he wouldn't follow. The last fact meant staying in a hard place on a boat well after lesser men and women with less time in were promoted. It was hard to do the right thing but never has the right thing happened to him. So hard is what he had to be.

"Here." From beneath the pile of pears in the bowl at the center of her table, she pulls an oversized onion. "Take this and rub it on your privates. Plant it next to a young oak on an island. If in two months the oak starts to lose its leaves, you'll know its youth transferred to the onion. Dig it back up. It doesn't matter if it started to grow or not. Cut it up in your bathtub and run hot water. Take a bath for the time it takes you to say three rosaries. You know how to say the rosary?"

Arlis can't answer. Of course, he doesn't know the rosary. But that's the least impossible part of his treatment plan. Second place goes to taking a bath with an onion. The smell would take a week to come off him. How would that get him any closer to finding someone? If a session of self-love with an onion wasn't enough, there's the burying by a young oak part. Not only did he think this whole thing would unravel when the young tree didn't lose a leaf, but to find a young, thriving tree in this sparse, soggy land would be impossible.

A cackle catches him by surprise, and he jumps backward in his chair, nearly toppling himself.

"You should see your face!" She continues to cackle and nearly chokes on her pear, her cheeks and neck turning raspberry. Arlis rises to help, but both the vertigo and the look coming from over the closed fist covering her mouth tell him to sit back down. She catches her breath and clears her throat. "Arlis, I don't know how to help you. I've never treated someone with that problem. My grandmother, she never passed that down." A breath escapes Arlis, another he didn't know he was holding. Against the backdrop of his shame, he hadn't noticed the hope growing. Sarah allowed him to think about his body, about touch, about a life he could live. But she cannot help him. His dashed hope leaves him angry, but not with her and her joke at his expense. It was foolish to think the hardness of life, ironically manifested in softness where it isn't wanted, could be reversed by this sad, lonely woman in a fairytale shack. He can't be angry at someone who wants to help him, unlike the sea, or the federal government, or his Coast Guard crew. Besides, she was able to tease an expression onto his face when the testing of the world could not. He looks at her hands, sporting wrinkles and strength, and wonders what it is like to help and have people feel it.

"Grandmother?" he asks, trying to move quickly past his disappointment. She doesn't seem annoyed by his questions anymore.

"Yeah. My grandmother taught me how to treat when I was around nine. I thought we were playing a silly doctor game with all my dolls. I didn't put it together until I was thirty-one. I had my calling in a dream. When I woke up, all I could think about was my grandmother and those doctor games. I remembered every one. But she never worked on the privates of my boy dolls. I can fix that dizziness for you, though."

"How'd you know about that?" In this strange conversation, it feels like they have been talking for years instead of minutes. Maybe the gunfire made things real, quickly. She's suspended the rules. It has to do with the black glass of her eyes softening as they talk. To look at them now, he sees the same weary compassion of the icons on her walls.

"I can help you," she offers.

"No," he says resolutely. Her eyebrows fly up. He came here to help, not to be helped. All he knows is she looks tired.

"You're my last patient."

"No," he says again.

Her quizzical look remains affixed to him while they sit in silence. A familiar piece of a hostage situation appears. Sarah wants to wait Arlis out, break his resolve. But Arlis knows it's not what she needs. After years of watching weary, pleading eyes he's become attuned to when someone needs something even if they can't say it. Reaching across the table, his fingers find her hand. He gently releases her grip from her cup and goes to the pot of reheated syn coffee on the wood stove in the corner. This stove is out of place in this world, but exactly where it should be. He pours without spilling a drop. Doing so shows him the vertigo hasn't returned. He somehow knows how she takes her coffee: honest, with no cream, no sugar. The cup returns to her hand, and he finds his place across from her again.

"Now. What can I help *you* with?" Arlis stares deep into her eyes, diving in headlong with not a flinch.

"What?" she says, her brow furrowing.

"What?" Arlis asks, not able to look away from her black pools anymore.

"This…isn't how it goes."

"I said the same thing," Arlis remembers as he locks his eyes on hers, "when I realized what the Coast Guard really is. I went in thinking I would be saving lives and helping people. I'd be part of something greater. Many I couldn't save, people and things I couldn't protect. One day my job became bigger than me and bigger than the reasons I started doing it. Helping is really a matter of opinion. The people who need the most help rarely get to decide what'd be helpful." His head shakes with the last phrase, as if all the memories of incorrect helping are droplets still clinging to his wet head. Sun peeks through the clouds and races through the windows, meeting Sarah's eyes. Brown appears at the edges of her irises, something Arlis is sure had not been there before. The brown intensifies, as if something old and buried in deep soil is rising to the surface. "What help do you need?" he asks.

Arlis can almost see the memories coming the surface of her eyes. He watches her life play out there, waiting for her to tell him what she did not get, could not be, or was not able to let go of. Instead, her eyes harden again as she switches back to her role as a waiting healer. He softens his gaze to a smile, something he has not felt on his face in uncountable years. Her face softens as well before she speaks.

"I was married once. In my twenties. It was a bad idea. At least we could both admit it. But it took seven years. Seems we spend our twenties reconciling the outside to our inside, trying to make everyone else see what only we can see. In my thirties, I decided I needed to reconcile the inside to the outside. What had been on my inside was confusing. Life made things real. I didn't. That's when the calling happened. I gave my life over to God and to treating. It was easy. It meant no more being confused. I had my job—my mission. But three years ago, I got sick. I tried using treatments on myself, but they weren't working. I didn't have anything left for me. I'd given it all away. So, I asked Jesus to take a break. And when he and the Virgin didn't say anything, I figured they thought it was ok. The sickness got better for a while, but it's back lately. I can't ever seem to eat. That pear was the first thing I've been hungry for in weeks." The brown in her eyes lighten. A cryptic smile spreads on her face. After a moment he deciphers the look, knowing it only as the one he, too, has coveted: relief.

"Arlis? Are you crying?"

With little practice having expressions, his face twists in pain, then in joy, as tears saunter down his cheeks. Sarah's smile widens before standing and straightening herself. He swears he's looking at another, younger woman. She looks taller, like the years of burden have been pulled from her shoulders. Only a trace of weariness is left in her eyes now. As the normally absent sun streams through the window to find her full figure, she glows and says "You've paid me with a listening ear. I'm going to treat your dizziness now."

Arlis doesn't protest anymore. He wonders how long he could remain in her company. The thought of being her helper, however that works for her, soothes him in a way all the thank you meals from the marsh mamas never could. She moves behind him, standing above his seated body, and places a hand on each side of his head as if about to gently cradle it, but keeps her hands several inches from his ears.

"Close your eyes and breathe deep." Had he not seen her walk behind him he'd swear she was speaking from just in front of his face. He does as he's told. As his eyes close, he feels her hands enter his ears and squeeze. She mutters her prayer, and her hands travel deeper within his body, past the places of the vertigo, through his neck and chest. He feels life sprout through every place her fingers travel. As her hands pass his pelvis to reach for his feet, he feels something stir between his legs.

In the Absence of Words

Cajuns, along with some Creole settlers of color, made their bedding from the dried Spanish moss, so named by the indigenous people in their comparison of this cousin of the pineapple to the beards of Spanish colonizers. This stuff, which still hangs from trees all the way up to Illinois, was found throughout Southern Louisiana. Many of our recovered photo archives of old Louisiana mansions, pre-Hurricane Pilar, have moss hanging from trees, creating tunnels of foliage leading up to corrupt plantation homes. Again, in history, we see how the keepers of the earth knew the true value of these plants, while the rich saw them only as decoration. What do you think Mr. Michot?"

"Pauvre bête."

"Could not have said it better myself. Come back next week to the Cajun/Creole in the 21ˢᵗ podcast, a subsidiary of YouTube History USA, and find out about the Atakapa-Ishak. Until then, please subscribe and like us, but more importantly, respect and cherish."

Jamil clicks off the mics and smiles at Michot.

"That was another good one. We can get furniture and bedding advertisers. In fact, I even know of a friend in the bamboo bedding business I can call."

"Mais, dat sounds good, yeah." Michot says, beginning a wet, semi-staged cough. "Dat'll be a good ting," he continues to cough out, hoping Jamil won't ask him the same thing as last week.

"You sure you're not ready to narrate the whole thing? If you're too worried about people understanding you, I can subtitle it. I just think it's disrespectful."

"Mais, I tole you. Dis French ain't like France French. It's hard to translate dat. And some Cajun words don't make sense in English."

"And I told *you*, Mr. Michot, I can pop out an algorithm in half an hour that can translate anything." Jamil's offer feels to Michot just like everything else on this show: a warm challenge. The young man's dreadlocks shake as he nods his head in anticipation.

"I see how hard you work on dis show. You don't need no extra work. Anyway, I don't like to be too long from my friends at da hippy house. Dey give me *misère* if I stay out."

Jamil chuckles and stands. When Michot stands, he notices for the first time that Jamil is the same height as him, a short 5'6", though Jamil is wider. "Alright, Mr. Michot. Let's get you back to your co-op."

Michot feels bad lying. Jamil has done more for him than anyone since Pilar when he was nine. Even at that age, he knew he'd be left with nothing and no one after they invented Category 6 just for that storm. When a moment of shared remembrance of The Storm happened with someone, he would pantomime the deep loss for them. But for him it was not for the past, but of a future and lives that never got lived. Jamil makes him feel like there could be a future again.

Much of his living is still in the past in The Duck Capital of the World: Gueydan, Louisiana. Before the town succumbed to the Gulf, the crawfish in the ponds didn't need to be responsibly farmed or organic. Crawfish eat shit, after all. People weren't piled on top of each other like they tend to be now. Michot was rich in nature and poor in people. His nearest neighbor (really the only person he could call a neighbor) on one of America's stubbornly unpaved roads, lived three quarters of a mile away. Michot's parents told him that the people at the end of the road lived there for a reason and there was no cause to disturb their self-imposed exile. He didn't quite understand what that made him, being he lived second to last on a dirt road to nowhere in 2025. The lack of TV, internet, or phone privileges added to his confusion over who was in exile. The only difference he could see was that his father at least travelled the road enough to kill the grass, while the way to the neighbors was nearly overgrown.

On a hot August day that year, a young boy paddled a homemade pirogue, silent as an incoming fog, through the shallow crawfish pond next to Michot's house. Michot thought at first it must be one of the farmers. It was always a treat to see the men working from their little boats. Michot would wave as they passed back and forth, until his mother would call him inside to scold him. Seeing another kid, who was not one of his six adopted siblings, was beyond special. The dark-eyed, dark-haired boy peered at him from his flat-bottomed canoe, hidden behind azalea bushes. That was as much of an invitation for conversation as Michot needed.

"Hi," Michot said, eight times. It started out as a failed whisper and ended as a shout. His feet brought him closer and closer though he knew they shouldn't. His mother would hear and see, but he didn't care. The stranger, dressed in clothes recycled several times, startled with each "hi." On the eighth one, it was the new kid, not his mother who scolded him.

"*Tais toi!*" Michot smiled widely at the sound of a voice he hadn't heard before, and even wider to hear something other than English. "Poo-yie you talk a lot!"

"Hi! I'm a Michot. I'm adopted. I have six brothers and sisters. What's your name? How many brothers and sisters do you have?"

The youth lowered his eyes and looked back across the pond, squinting toward an unknown sight. He looked back at Michot. "My daddy, he tinks I'm fishing out behind ma house. I have to go." Because his mother never called to him that day, he could watch the new boy paddle away between the orange rings of the crawfish traps until he couldn't see him any longer.

MICHOT REPLAYS THE FIFTY-YEAR-OLD memory several more times over the week. His co-op roommates check on him as he tends to stare out of the window longer than usual. They likely believe he is thinking about the show and his time with Jamil, the only thing he's ever spoken about for more than three seconds. At bedtime, he'll hold his cup of tea halfway to his mouth, caught between the present and the past. Sometimes the roommates touch his shoulder to rouse him. But when Jamil arrives, harkening the new episode to be recorded, Michot finds himself solidly in the present.

"Mr. Michot a lot of people love learning about Cajuns and Creoles from you. Our podcast has as many subscribers as the regional Catahoula Cur Lovers podcast. That's unheard of! Some comments are even from YouTube History International. Several are from the French Republic of the European Union, Canada, and the state of Congo in Africa."

"*Je n'sais pas.*"

"You gotta tell me, did everyone talk Cajun French when you were growing up?"

"*Non. Non.* Most people weren't talking French no more. Just a few holdouts. People who lasted."

"Lasted. I like that. Maybe you could talk about that in the next episode, take a bigger part of this."

"*Mais,* I tought we talked about dis. I'm just here to put some spice on dat."

"You need to read the comments. People are asking for more of you. I mean, most of the stuff we talk about people could easily search the internet for. It's you, your voice, your outlook, they can't find on the internet."

"It's like dey say: *Ils déchirent le gingat.*"

"Uh-huh. Well, you just let me know. We really don't need a special topic. I mean, you're the whole show."

Jamil smiles warmly, his grin toothy and handsome. When he'd come looking through co-ops and retirement homes seeking someone who still had the old language, Michot didn't say anything. The other lonely souls fawned over Jamil. His good looks, his energy, his respect, and his easy attitude were all coveted commodities, intoxicating enough to stop remembering life and instead want to live it again. At first that's why Michot thought he coughed up the old accent, wrapping his Rs and singing his As. As he listened to the rhythm of that speech tumbling from his mouth, rhythm reminiscent of the waves the Cajuns had been cast into not once, but now twice in history, he felt a part of him rise from a decades long slumber. Jamil listened, laughed, and was curious, coaxing from Michot something he was sure died in the aftermath of Pilar. Because of Jamil's warm, mahogany eyes, Michot could no longer be sure he'd indeed heard the last words spoken in the Cajun language.

Michot watches as Jamil paints the picture of the Atakapas for the new episode. The French and Spanish both saw them as threatening savages. Stories of their cannibalism did nothing for the perceived threat, expediting their extermination. Jamil speaks of them with the same warmth and reverence he always seems to carry for the peaceful. He wears defiance for those who would try to tear them down. Both tones are present as he talks about the last Atakapa speaker dying sometime in the 1940s, nearly 150 years ago. Michot wonders what that poor person felt like to talk about his world with words only he understood.

In the past, Michot's own world had been created by words he'd tell trees and birds, the only creatures who seemed to want to listen. After a week of not seeing his visitor, little Michot thought his chance to touch the world outside of their acre and a half had passed into oblivion like an old Atakapa-Ishak speaker. But the young boy arrived again one evening at dusk, barely visible in his pirogue from behind the kudzu enveloping the young red oak at the edge of the Michot property. While he knew he should care about what his family would think if he slipped away, he couldn't stop the questions from coming out.

"Where'd you go last time you left? How long have you been there? Do you live close? Do you have any toys? Do you want to come inside and play?"

The patchwork boy's dark brow furrowed somewhere between confusion and frustration.

"*Mon Dieu.* You talk so much."

"Mother says that, too. She says I was quieter than any of my other siblings when they were adopted. She doesn't understand why I'm so talkative now. She said she chose me because I was a quiet baby. What's your name?"

"'tit-Claude."

"Hi T-Claude. Do you want to play?"

"Babies play."

"Babies play with baby things. We can play like nine-year-olds. Wait, are you nine?"

"Eight."

"I'm older than you. Don't you want to play?"

T-Claude looked at him seriously, furrowing his brow again. "I don't have time, me. Why you wanna play so much? You don't got work to do?"

"I do my home school lessons in the mornings. Mother says play is part of my homework and she'd rather me do it outside."

"I like outside. I get more tings done dere."

"Why do you talk like that?"

"*Mais*, why you talk like dat?"

"Mother says speaking intelligently is part of the path to intelligence."

T-Claude eyed him suspiciously. Was it because Michot spoke without his same accent? Or was it because he didn't know how to work a pirogue?

"I gotta go. My daddy will want dese frogs fried up before dark," T-Claude finally said.

"You eat frogs? Ewwwwww…"

T-Claude smiled as only an eight-year-old who'd grossed out another kid could smile. "You should see when I find some nutra to put in da gumbo."

"What's a 'nutra'? Is it like a bear? Or a dragon?"

There were so many reasons for T-Claude to never come back this way. Michot had never lived off the land. It's clear he had no family other than the collection of siblings in his house. Now he asked if a nutria rat is similar to bears or dragons the way one would ask if a Po-boy is like a sandwich. But T-Claude smiled again because everyone knows catching dragons for a gumbo is more fun than work.

"*Tu n'es pas fou, mais tu fais drôle.*"

"What's that mean?"

"I'll come back, *cher.*"

T-CLAUDE'S WORDS ECHO throughout Jamil's episode of the disappeared Atakapas. Michot tries to distill thoughts, distill emotions, distill life the way T-Claude could do with just a phrase. He wishes he could make sense of the past and this land for Jamil, giving him words to depict a world before it was washed away. He's unsure if he'd ever find those words in any language since he has almost always felt like a visitor himself.

"And as in most stories of colonization and extermination of indigenous people in America, our forefathers decided to assuage their guilt by naming places in the region after these noble people. In this case it was a wilderness trail. What say you to that Mr. Michot?"

"*Mauvaise partance, bonne arrivée.*"

"That's it for today's episode. Next week we'll look at how Catholic religion shaped governance, yes I said governance, so much that people here named their municipal districts 'parishes.' Until then, please subscribe and like us, but more importantly, respect and cherish."

The projected screen with the script before them goes dark, as do the lights on the mics. Since Pilar, Michot has always initiated silences, relished in them when others would have to fill the hungry void with meaningless talk. When Jamil showed up wanting to listen, giving purpose for words again, Michot broke his own dam so the words, memories, and meaning, could flood back. His days are filled with daydreams; his evenings are spent talking to himself in French, trying to remind his mouth. All the while, he feels as if he is being unearthed, a crusty old crawfish coming up from the mud, having spent too many winters hiding. When the silence appears between the two men, his newly flooded soul can't tolerate it, and he must investigate.

"You alright, T-boy?" Michot's asks Jamil in a large, Cajun volume. It diminishes at the end out of respect for the broken silence.

"Me? Of course. This stuff is just…heavy."

"*Ouias.*" More silence follows. Michot feels uneasiness ripple through him like a wind across the crawfish pond. "*Mais* dere's a lot tings we had to say goodbye to. But we…" He stops. It's his job to finish that sentence. He is the old man, required to impart wisdom. The problem is he doesn't know what happens after goodbyes, other than silence. "Trute is I don't know 'but what.'"

"Me neither."

The silence gnaws at Michot. He wants so much for Jamil to smile warmly and bring life back to the room. It's irritating how this quiet has become his enemy again—the way it was in his adoptive house. Returning to the immobility of his youth (pre-T-Claude) reminds him of how he managed silences then: be as helpful, as curious, and as talkative as the other person could tolerate. He's been helpful. His curiosity is what led him into this whole process. Could it be time to be talkative? Michot knows what Jamil wants. The young man's happiness is worth more than his insecurity about language.

"Tell you what, *cher*. I'll do you whole nex show. I'll say da whole ting."

"Seriously?"

"You gotta tell me what to say, dough."

"You don't worry about that. That will be covered."

Jamil's energy blasts back through the makeshift studio. On the car ride home, his happy questions return and Michot settles into his old silence. Except it's not settling. His craving for reconnection with Jamil made him promise something he couldn't possibly deliver. The reality of his impulsive decision sinks in. Throwing out a phrase here and there is not the same as expounding in the old language on Cajun life, culture, or much worse, family history. Dread sets in as Jamil cheerfully drops him off at the co-op.

Michot skips dinner to work on words. He scrolls through memories looking for the sounds and experiences he knows Jamil expects. His mind stops on an image of T-Claude in a tree shouting down to him.

"*MAIS, NON!* YOU CAIN'T come up here, *boug*."

"Mesopotamia!"

"Dat's not even a word. You made dat up!"

"I didn't! It's a place where it's believed civilization started."

T-Claude dropped to the ground, soundless, like a cat. He still didn't quite get play concepts like needing a password to join someone in a tree. "You say I talk funny?"

"It's really a place. Or it was."

"You ever seen it?"

"No. But I don't have to. I can imagine it."

"*Bête comme un bête a chandelle.* Why you 'imagine' so much?"

"Because it makes me happy. You don't do it? How do you get happy?"

T-Claude eyed him seriously again, checking if the question was really meant to be answered. "When I ride my four-wheeler to mah cousins to get Daddy's beer from dem, it makes me happy. When I'm full, and I cooked someting mah daddy likes, I'm happy. On Saturdays, when mah daddy drinks more beer, he tells me about mah momma before she got sick and went to heaven. He tells me about before his accident on da oil rig, when we could buy tings."

Little Michot looked down and then back at his house. Still, no one from his family appeared to scold him. He was beginning to believe they liked him gone.

"Let's go build a fort. In those trees over there."

It was the first game Michot had come up with which T-Claude didn't struggle to understand. They worked, together, to construct one of the most elaborate forts eight and nine-year-olds should be able to make. All the while, T-Claude gave instructions, shared ideas, and even brainstormed imaginary amenities. It was a type of practical play Michot had never done before. It was productive. Their worlds mixing made something new. To mix like this left Michot feeling seen and understood. It was better than the two hours his mother spent teaching him, and the twenty minutes his siblings would tolerate playing with him before his mother walked out of earshot. Despite his comments about how much Michot talked, T-Claude wanted to immerse Michot in his world, and he wanted in Michot's; a shared intimacy a nine-year-old knows without the clumsiness of words. Once done with their fort, the boys both looked at it lovingly.

"I like dat, me," T-Claude breathed out. Michot stood next to him, panting and sweating as well.

"What should we do in it?"

"I'll be a mechanic. You roll dat four-wheeler in here."

Michot looked around for the four-wheeler T-Claude always talked about but realized there was only the pirogue he'd silently ridden up in, hidden against the little levee behind some bushes. Michot gave his friend a clueless look. T-Claude's eyes rolled with frustration, maybe at how long it was taking Michot to bring the imaginary contraption in to be worked on. "*Mais, la. Allons!*"

"*MAIS, LA. ALLONS!*" MICHOT SAYS against the silence draping over his body. His friend's words, said in the present, lighten the world around him. He doesn't know how he'll be able to channel enough of the past to make it through a whole podcast. The words feel foreign now, like he's saying everything wrong. But Jamil doesn't know that. Jamil doesn't even care. Michot wonders if the last Atakapa-Ishak speaker really knew what he was saying. Who would know the difference?

By the time Jamil's energy fills the co-op again, and the heart of every person he passes, Michot feels ready. Doing this for Jamil, even though it goes against the years of silence he has accumulated since Pilar, is right. The attempts he'd made to find friends, and even lovers, who'd want to be in his world and whose world he'd want to be in, never worked. Not until Jamil found him. Michot tells jokes on the car ride to the studio. Jamil's eyes sparkle while his whole-body laughs, concerning himself not at all with the unbridled vulnerability of his joy. It cuts away forty-nine silent years at the speed of happiness.

Michot pulls up to the mic with particular energy. He's ready to talk, to watch each word, each intonation, draw Jamil deeper in. He'll talk about religion, governance, or dragons:

whatever it takes to dive deeper into a world he can both share and be wanted in.

Instead of turning toward the screen for his script, Jamil clicks on a mic over his own shoulder and faces Michot. "All right folks. It's the moment you've been asking for. Mr. Michot has decided he's going to talk with us. Today there won't be any looks back to the influence of Catholicism on Cajuns. Because we have the living, breathing culture in front of us. So, I give you the most interesting topic of this series: Mr. Michot."

Blood evacuates Michot's body and he becomes cold. A weight drops through his stomach and is headed to the earth's core. Jamil sees all of it and cuts off the microphones.

"You ok?"

Michot stares, seeing Jamil through a tunnel. He watches Jamil's mouth move, but the voice is T-Claude's. T-Claude's face paints over Jamil's and is dirtier than usual. The young Cajun boy looked tired as he stared out over the completely dried up crawfish pond.

"It's gonna be *mauvais, mauvais.*" He looked at Michot then. "Dat means bad. See how dis pond all dried up and cracked like dat? Daddy says all da water been sucked out in da gulf and left dis hot behind."

"Yes. Mother says we will be leaving tomorrow. I get to pack a bag."

"Y'all be cahful."

"Where are you going?"

"Me. Right here. I been nailing boards to ma house. Daddy cain't go nowhere. He's too hurt, him."

"You can come with us."

"I cain't leave my daddy, *cher.* He needs my help."

"The weather reports say the storm surge will overtake Pecan Island. Some say it could even be strong enough to push seawater here. And even if the water doesn't get here, the winds are 189 miles per hour and—"

"You just keep talking. We'll survive. Daddy says dat's what we do best. You a Michot. Dat sounds Cajun. Dat means you'll survive."

"Michot is my adopted name."

T-Claude looked him over, from his blond hair and blue eyes, to his slender legs, like he was seeing it all for the first time. "You feel Cajun to me."

The dark boy's olive skin is replaced by Jamil's umber face. His mouth continues to move and his words become discernible.

"…and that means there can't be any wrong answers to this. We all want what you know. We all just want…you." There's a panic in Jamil's look, like watching someone held above a maelstrom with their fingers slipping. If there can't be a wrong answer, why is he afraid? There is no way to fact check his story, and the language is as utilized as Latin though not as studied (much less written). What's left? The absence of a story is all. Michot's life did not have the twists or turns anyone would find interesting. A Levee Technician's work is silent steps to find breaches in the safety of the levees. He would not have wished that work, or his whole life, on someone. What life would he have wanted? What life would people who watch this want to see? There's only one other life he'd ever been able to know.

"*C'est* OK. *Je suis prêt.* Turn on you micraphone."

Jamil looks safe from the maelstrom. He presses the button over his shoulder and settles into his seat. He's beaming.

"Mr. Michot, can you tell us about what it was like growing up in a Cajun household?"

"*Mais* it was a lot mo work den you tink. I was always fishing and hunting for *ma famille.* Den I'd have to cook it all."

"Cook? How old were you when you learned to cook?"

"Must have been sometime before I was eight."

"Eight! No way! What were you cooking at eight?"

"*Les ouaouarons.* Dat's frogs."

"Frogs. So you really lived off of the land."

"Yeah, we had to. My momma died when I was *petit*. My daddy got hurt on da rigs. My cousins could help, dough."

"I imagine family was an important part of the culture in South Louisiana before the floods."

"*Oui*. Family was you world. You din't do nothing without you family."

"What did you and your family do during Hurricane Pilar?"

Michot feels blood try to leave him again. He loses his grip on the words. This is where the life he wanted to live ends. More accurately, this is where T-Claude leaves him. Michot never wanted to be T-Claude. He just wanted to keep him, be seen by him, and share life. It should be T-Claude to be the last speaker, the language leaving with him. Jamil's eyes look again from the mouth of a maelstrom. He couldn't save T-Claude then. Nine-year-olds who have been collected by their adults, as T-Claude put it "like tractor parts," aren't able to do such things. But he can save Jamil from this disappointment with the last piece of T-Claude he has. In the process he can make his only friend live on, even if it's for a little while.

"*Mais* we tru us a hurricane party. It was big big."

"A hurricane party?"

"We cleaned out da freezer and ate til we was…*grassel*. Wasn't long after dat da *vente* started blowing. Me and my daddy tought we wasn't gonna make out."

"How did you make out?"

"Dat old house was on tick beams…*tu compren*? A big gust pushed the house off the pillars and we started floating. It must've been God who did dat because if da house had not have moved with da currents and da wind it would have been like my Daddy say: *A vos soigne ton char comme un char a nous autres.*"

"What's that?"

"Means we would have been past dead."

For nearly two hours Michot expounds on a life that should have been lived. After the storm he resettled the family site with money from FEMA. His father had a painless death, having let go of his grief and the accompanying alcoholism. The story continues through a successful professional career as a mechanical engineer. The anecdotes have both Jamil and Michot with tears in their eyes from the laughter. In love, too, this life was rich. Stories of lovers and a daughter who moved north, like all the other young folk in search of work, have them smiling contentedly. Finally, Michot tells of a friend, quiet and lonely, who came alive because of their relationship. After years of silence, this friend was able to find his voice and words to explain joy. Weeping as he talks about what this friend meant, he sees Jamil mirroring him. Jamil wipes his eyes and turns off the microphones.

"Thank you, Mr. Michot. Thank you. This is amazing." Michot wipes his own eyes in time to see Jamil's strong young torso press against him in an embrace.

Everyone in the co-op notices the difference in Michot. He talks to all of them, barely letting them get a word in edgewise. He has time to make up for. Words flow out of him at such a rate that some of the roommates start to avoid him. Experience reminds him to give them a little space, and they will come back. In talking, he gets to hear so much more than before. Sharing stories means he can see all the places he was not alone, the times when his life was, in fact, nice. By the time Jamil comes to pick him up the following week he can hardly contain his excitement. Bouncing into the car he greets the young man happily.

"*Bonjour* Jamil! We gonna have us a large time today!"

"Hi, Mr. Michot."

His words and tone fall flat. It's like that day he felt "heavy" talking about the Atakapa-Ishak, but much, much worse. Jamil's mahogany eyes won't come up to meet Michot's blue ones.

"Why you *bouder, cher?* Huh? Why you bottom lip out like dat?"

"You don't know what you're saying."

"*Mais*, yeah. I really do want to know why you sad."

"No. You don't know what you're saying in Louisiana French."

Blood no longer exists for Michot. He turns old and weighted, like the wet boards of T-Claude's destroyed house finally caught up to bury him, too.

"I made that algorithm I told you about and used it on last week's episode. When you cleaned out the freezer for your hurricane party, you ate until you were *grassel*. Which means you ate until you were a towhee or ground robin, a bird that used to be indigenous to these parts. And when the *vente* blew…I think you meant *vent*. Because *vente* is an auction. Or a sale. Like at a store. And when you asked '*tu compren*' you must have meant '*tu comprends*' because what you said didn't even make sense."

"Dat's just some mispronunciations."

"I'd hoped so, given there are so few people for you to speak with. But when the wind moved your house, and your father said you would have been past dead: *A vos soigne ton char comme un char a nous autres*…after some tweaking, the algorithm showed it meant 'We'll treat your car like it's our own.' And the rest of the transcript only gets worse from there."

Silence falls between them. Michot looks at his feet the same way he did in the windowless van as his adopted family left Gueydan for Illinois. This stint in the land of the living with Jamil will have to carry him from here to the end of his life the way his time with T-Claude carried him to here. He looks up to Jamil a last time.

"Why'd you do it?" Jamil asks.

It would be infinitely easier to remain in the silence, oppressive yet predictable, than venture an attempt at an explanation. But there is just enough of the warm challenge in his voice, paired with the same tone of frank acknowledgement T-Claude would use, that he cannot help but let himself be seen.

"Someone talked to me like this once. Only friend I ever had. He's gone now. This is all that's left of him. And you wanted me to share it. You remind me of him. I got caught up in it all." His words carry none of the soft vowels, replaces none of the "th" sounds with "d." His voice is more foreign than ever.

Jamil leans forward, placing his face in his hands. Rocking back and forth makes his anguish apparent. Michot realizes he did the one thing Jamil stands against: robbing someone of their history, their culture, and their identity. He can hear Jamil breathing through his fingers, either trying to calm himself or prepare a litany of completely true indictments. Jamil sits straight up, looks at the ceiling for a moment, and then levels his gaze on Michot.

"Then I guess you're all we got."

Michot responds with a silent question on his face.

"Who I need to interview is your friend. Everywhere else I've looked, there's just pieces. You're the closest I've come to finding the real thing. So you'll have to do. I'm going to be honest; you've wasted my time and the time of the people who subscribe. You owe them an explanation. A real one."

There is no warmth in this challenge. Michot knows he doesn't deserve it. Jamil should've been able to meet T-Claude. Like him, Jamil wants to be in T-Claude's world, and have him here in his. Searching Jamil's face for some understanding, memory again blends with the present. The face of the little boy, the one who stole moments to play, and ended up remaking Michot's world with both words and silence, superimposes over Jamil's. The dark boy sits in his pirogue, dirty as ever, with dark clouds in the Gulf behind him. A smile, bigger than any one Michot had seen in life, spreads across his face.

"Mr. Michot?"

"Call me Ben."

Lite Enough

Her daddy said a strong man is not measured by the height of his fence, or how far his gun can shoot, but by how long he builds his table. Maybe nowadays he'd say it's about how big a boat he keeps because of all the water. But Lenae always wondered how big a table she would need to build to be a strong woman. She'd be happy if she could be the glue of the community using food the way her grandmother did. That's why she likes these pop-up food truck festivals. In addition to serving restaurant regulars, like soft-eyed Mr. Boudreaux, she gets to interact with a larger community, more as a friend than a businesswoman. Her small mouth smiles broadly as she passes food through the window of her cousin's borrowed second gen electric food truck. Lenae wears the most recent fashions to these get-togethers. While she normally doesn't bother with makeup in her hot kitchen, she puts on lab made walnut tinted base and bright red lipstick. She always wears her bouncy, curly hair done up for the festivals. This is partially to add a much-needed feeling of youthful charm to these festivals, but mostly so no one would peg her as a woman who's endured so much loss. The pain of the past melts away like makeup in her kitchen when she makes the whole capital city her table to share the love. She knows her grandmother and father would approve, but it doesn't feel like enough.

One white man eats more than others. His square jaw and pointed nose sit above a perfectly round belly, growing as he takes in the day's fare, despite the tailored shirt attempting to hide it. He doesn't seem to mind how out of place he is but isn't trying to call attention to himself. The shirt also attempts to hide his age, which Lenae places in his mid-forties, like her. On the man's third trip around the booths, she notes his choice of carbon fiber clothes and fine vinyl shoes. They stand out among the cotton blend tee shirts and rubber boots of Natchitoches.

"What's your name?" Lenae finally asks him, keeping her voice sweet and curious.

"Rhys Driessen," he says with a startled look as if he'd thought he camouflaged.

"Mr. Driessen, you either have a hole in your stomach, or you've never been to a Louisiana festival before." She shifts in the mud, her white rubber boots slurping as they sink.

"It's rare I get to eat food with real meat products in it. This is amazing."

"Well, honey, this is just the Rice Festival. Even if we have to make our rice from daikon radish, we're still going to celebrate it. We moved it up here, all the way in Natchitoches because…you know. You should come for the Cochon de Lait Festival."

"A Pig Festival! They told me you do things differently down here. This is amazing. Your food is special. It's so complex. Have you thought about having a restaurant?"

Lenae's bright teeth shimmer in the overcast and her mahogany eyes sparkle. They've been saying that about her family's cooking for generations. That question is what caused her grandmother to open their restaurant in the first place.

"I do. You're welcome to come to my place, Hendricks' Creole and Soul Food, right up the road. But eat up here and now. You couldn't eat like that at my restaurant for free."

She cocks one of her generous hips and juts her soft chin into the air to show she means business.

"Let me give you my e-card." He shakes his watch to get ready to flick his info in her direction.

"I left my phone in the car."

"You don't have an implant? Or even a cell watch?"

"No, Mr. Driessen. I only keep a handheld. Don't trust that wearable technology or implant stuff. Too expensive anyway." She almost explains how the insurance for her restaurant leaves her with no funds for frivolous things like the outpatient procedure an implant requires, but Mr. Driessen's condescending smirk stops her. It's one Lenae has seen before, but the accompanying confusion—or curiosity—makes it all look weird. "You got to remember," she offers, "we're not a place where cutting edge happens. Never will be, either. But that's what allows us to do things no one else can anymore."

"I'd love to see and taste more. I'll be by tomorrow after I've had a chance to digest."

Lenae smiles to herself as she packs her truck. Her cousins notice. She figures they're hoping she hit it off with the out-of-towner. They don't think she's social enough. Lenae looks so lonely in her restaurant. But her cousins watched her life shrink when her parents died. All her solitude has done is minimize the potential to be disappointed, rather than refill her life until it could be enough again. But she always takes a shining to new people. Maybe it's the novelty: a new belly to fill and a new heart to feel the love of her family's flavors. Sharing a place at the table has always seemed enough for Lenae.

Food is for celebration, for mourning, for every physical ailment—including being full (you just change what you eat instead of stopping). At twelve, when the hormones of womanhood, paired with a table overflowing with red beans and (real) rice, homemade sausage, and even beignets, she began to fill out quickly. While the rest of her parents' generation were becoming solidly vegan and vegetarian, her family staged a rebellion by doubling down on food the rest of the country tasted as "inhumane" and "ignorant." As if America had not already found enough reasons to pathologize being big and full, it is now taken as a sign of someone disrespecting the needs of others. She felt perpetually stuck between the ideals of her generation and her region about what is enough. Lenae worked for years to reconcile her family's form of love and the way it ultimately hurt others. But Lenae's compromise to love her family despite their ways eroded with the funeral of one parent and ended completely at the other's. After that, the thought of altering their recipes was like altering her memory of them. It made her the last one interested in making dishes the old way. With all the hours of love going into and coming out of these dishes, for these people, her life was full enough.

The day after the festival she opens her restaurant early, making sure there won't be an excuse for the visitor to skip town without stopping in. If he wanted to taste, she would make sure his tongue would have more than enough. She makes specials, dishes she'd only make during holidays or big family gatherings. There are red beans with tasso and duck and andouille gumbo. Meat pies, a local favorite that survived the inundation of migrants from South Louisiana, lay in a golden-brown mound at the end of the table. She makes the most renowned dish—turkey neck jambalaya. That special had been on the chalkboard behind the register since her grandmother wrote it there the morning of the day she died. Lenae, and her parents before her, made it every day since, in loving memory of Granny Cece.

The lunch crowd trickles and then floods in. She's got her head down, sweat gathering on her dark walnut skin, spooning together plate lunches when Mr. Boudreaux's big puppy brown eyes glance over her shoulder into the kitchen.

"I smell that turkey neck jambalaya."

"That's not ready to be served yet, Mr. Boudreaux."

"Then who's it waitin' for? You could put me some in a cup and no one would notice."

"Here's what I got right now. Come back later if you want it so much."

"Come on, Lenae. You got three pots on magnet burners back there. Why you holdin' out on me?"

She shoos him away, his big brown eyes forlorn. His olive skin reddens from Lenae's uncharacteristic briskness. Just as the feeding frenzy (a line looped down through the gravel parking lot) threatens to erode her resolve, Mr. Driessen comes through the door. "Alright, y'all. Calm down," she tells the crowd before bringing the jambalaya from out back.

She gives Mr. Driessen her three specials on the house despite previously telling him otherwise. She thinks she is discreet, but Mr. Boudreaux and her other regulars are paying attention. They don't say anything to her, except for a cross look from Boudreaux. Instead, the regulars let the rest of the town know Hendrick's is serving all the good stuff. She has a line into the road in minutes. Her Venmo account is at a full day's worth of Bitcoin by the time she walks away from the thermo table. She approaches Driessen who is feverishly texting on a roll-up interface.

"Did you get enough?" Lenae asks.

"I don't know if I could ever get enough, Mrs…"

"Hendricks. Lenae Hendricks." She wags her head with pride so that her thick shoulder length curls bounced. The pride is partly for the name, but mostly for the compliment of her cooking.

"So, I haven't had a chance to tell you about who I am and what I do because you are so in demand around here. I'm a chef."

"I thought your name sounded familiar." Lenae's curls bounce again.

"I'm familiar in a lot of places. And I think you could be, too. No one cooks this food anymore. I think you could go big."

Lenae cautiously leans away. This is not at all what she bargained for. She wanted to bring more to her table, not bring her table to more. All the good feelings she got from the compliments of her cooking dissipate in the face of the unknown, where she can't be sure what she does in the kitchen would be enough.

"Mr. Driessen, you flatter. But I don't think anyone is going to like this food outside of Mississippi and Louisiana. You don't think they're going to look down their nose at it?"

"Yes, several people will. But society is starting to loop back to food trends from just before the turn of the century. Back then the more culturally obscure, the more the critics turned their nose up at it, the more it was in demand."

Not sure if was a backhanded compliment, she asks, "Ok... but what about the meat?" She is still leaning away, eyes narrowing in skepticism.

He smiles amusedly, or maybe hungrily. It's hard to tell. "Meat. Yeah. We're coming full circle. Just like how the environmental practices of the Fed shifted toward naturally occurring solutions, foodie menus are starting to do this, too. Our pre-human ancestors ate animal proteins, plain and simple. We are who we are because of the flesh we consume. It was essential to brain development. Our bodies have no limit to protein intake. It should be the real guiltless food." Lenae looks up at the restaurant, surveying her customers, making sure they have enough of what they came for. Driessen continues even without her mahogany eyes on him. "Plus, we can use everything on the animal. Even by-products and blood. It's the new 'natural' movement." His fingers motion the quotes as he squints.

"Mr. Driessen, I'm just a cook in a little plastic shack. This is poor people, country food. I don't know if I can do this somewhere else for anybody else."

"Mrs. Hendricks —"

"It's Miss."

Driessen smiles. Is it the single thing? Or because she interrupted and corrected him? Again, it's hard to figure out his face. People from outside Louisiana never seem to wear clear expressions to make you sure of how they feel. Because he'll likely be gone in a matter of hours like everyone else who finds themselves in Louisiana, she doesn't invest much time trying to intuit the enigma of his reactions.

"Miss Hendricks. I've been messaging people all over the world since yesterday. They know about you. They'll tell people. People will start coming here. You thought today was a feeding frenzy? You'll have more customers than you know how to handle."

Lenae's knees wobble and she sits. She nervously rubs her tired calves. Pulling herself upright in her chair, with a large breath inhaled, her eyes find her grandmother's handwriting advertising the perpetual special of turkey neck jambalaya. Some extra foot traffic from nearby states would be more than enough for her. This is not supposed to be a seam-busting business. And now, because this antsy white man decided to text his chef friends, the table she has built for her community won't be long enough to feed throngs of food tourists. She wonders how her father, or her grandmother, would handle this.

"I'm glad you think my food is good enough for all those people. But this is something I have to think about."

IT IS LENAE'S TURN TO HOST the Monday night card game for her cousins. She's never had to think about what they would eat. But the run on her restaurant wiped her out. She orders pizza. Two of her male cousins threaten to leave until some of the girls tell them they could stand to eat at least something vegetarian. Lenae reminds them she could have ordered from the vegan pizza chain instead. At first, she thinks the threat is enough to make them count their blessings. But she grows suspicious of the whispers coming from her girl cousins when they are followed by a hush. Anytime the talking stops in this family, it means they're mindful of ears. In this case, since she's the only one not smiling, she knows they're talking about her. Being left out of internal jokes is nothing new. An only child, unpartnered, and orphaned too early in life, means she's been a subject of many hushed conversations in this family. Frustrated, she lays her cards on the table and heads for the most comfortable room in the house: the kitchen. She busies herself with dishes while they carry on. She just about convinces herself there is nothing all that odd about how they're acting when Kiki sneaks beside her at the sink.

"Shit, girl! You scared me! Don't do that!" Lenae yells.

"Shhhh! What's going on with you and that white boy?"

"What white b—" she is interrupted with recognition. "That's why y'all are acting so stupid. That man is just some chef doing a food tour. He probably just wants to feature me on some YouTube channel like all those other ones."

"Mmmhmmm. I'm sure your food is all he was looking to taste and feature."

"Stop that, now," Lenae says, yanking the dishtowel from her shoulder to swat Kiki.

"C'mon, Lenae!"

"I said stop it."

"What'd he say to you, anyway?"

"He said I make good food."

"Mmmhmm. What else?"

"That's it."

"That ain't it. People saying y'all talked for longer than it takes to say, 'This sure is good grub, ma'am.'"The last few words were deeper in pitch.

"He don't talk like that." Lenae tries to say matter-of-factly but ends up sounding defensive.

Kiki smiles broadly. "What'd y'all talk about? He likes your food and…"

"…he's already told all his chef friends about it. Says he thinks it could go big."

"Lenae—" Kiki yells, but is cut short by Lenae's hand over her mouth, complete with a death look. Even though Kiki is older, her diminutive body size, short haircut, garish clothes, and gregarious nature, makes her seem like the little sister Lenae didn't get. Lenae becomes painfully aware of the silence at the card table.

"Y'all might as well all come in the kitchen so I can let all y'all down at once." She'd barely finished the sentence when the other eight cousins came forth from just behind the door. "Listen. Nothing is going to come from this. This nice chef who is really into food got excited and paid me a compliment. He probably forgot where Natchitoches is now that he's back in his big Dallas."

"Oh yeah?" Kiki asks while picking up Lenae's buzzing antique cellphone, and then waving for the cousins to see, Driessen's name digitally lit. "Then why did you program him in your old-ass phone? And why is he calling?"

Lenae looks at the phone and then back at Kiki's smug expression. Her cousins stare expectantly. The ringing stops without her answering it. It's her turn to look back smugly. She goes to open her mouth to remind them how short outsider's attention spans are when the phone rings again. Kiki answers.

"Hold on now, Mr. Driessen. She's right here." Kiki holds the phone out. Lenae takes the phone as if she were responding to a robocall advertising phone implants, though a nearly imperceptible shake in her legs betrays her attempt to appear indifferent. They all listen as Lenae has a brief conversation. There are lots of "yes's" and not a single "no." Her voice shakes as she agrees. She does wonder what other people are doing in their kitchens and she's always interested in making her cooking better. When she hangs up, Kiki jumps up and down, excited that her cousin decided to do something her parents, or their grandmother, would never do.

KIKI PROGRAMS THE CAR to a speed faster than Lenae is comfortable with. She doesn't want Lenae changing her mind before she can get her to Dallas. After a quick hand off to Driessen at DFW hyperloop terminal, Lenae finds herself whisked onto a long, suppository shaped train for Indianapolis. For years, she'd thought about getting on one of these to find herself in another part of the country in just a few hours. Getting as far as the purchase screen, she'd always talked herself out of it. The suddenness of a wish appearing, without her needing to purchase or plan, makes her even more skeptical. Driessen can sense this. His smile softens, even though his eyes do not. This trip, he reassures, is just to help her understand where her food fits in the world. Having never brought her family's cuisine beyond state lines, having watched the outside world only on screens, her curiosity wins over fear. They are in the tube, moving seven hundred miles an hour, before he tells her the full plan.

"Your gumbo needs to make a world debut. We're going to head to a couple of places so you can see how different chefs are doing soups lately. Silky is sexy when it comes to soups."

Lenae's eyebrows jump. "Gumbo isn't a soup," she corrects. "And my gumbo juice isn't silky?" Questionable silkiness in her gumbo somehow made her unsure if she was woman enough.

"Almost," Driessen says flatly. Lenae feels feeble. This is the first time in her life someone has said her food is not good enough. She's heard she wasn't thin enough. She's heard from her cousins she wasn't light skinned enough. When they were alive, her parents would say she is not dating enough, laughing enough, thinking enough, dreaming enough, or trying enough. Those standards didn't die with them. At least she heard her food is always enough for the first forty-three years of her life. That's been enough for her. Driessen lets loose this secret as if she's been lied to by the people she trusts the most. He continues without looking at her. "Your food is classic. It has so much flavor. But we have to get it up to speed with the other big players. And for that we need helium to lighten it up."

"Mr. Driessen, I don't think—"

"It's Rhys."

"Ok. Rhys, why do I need to get up to speed?" This is moving fast enough, she thinks. Driessen continues to stare forward, reticent, as he has throughout the conversation. She watches his face for expressions to help decipher what this is about. Lenae begins to plan on how to get a return ticket as soon as they arrive. To make an escape without drawing the wrath of some agenda she can smell but can't taste, she'll need to be both interested and aloof. "I don't know if I want to be with big players," her tone a concealed invitation, the way the spicy smell of jambalaya beckons you to look past it's mundane appearance, but ready to burn you if you don't respect it.

Now he turns toward her. "You don't know what you want. Two days ago at the festival, you didn't think you'd ever leave Louisiana, or ever want anything more than what you had. Yet, here you are." The corners of his mouth turn up as he looks her in the eye. His own eyes lay flat and expressionless. Calling her bluff so calmly stirs her vigorously.

In downtown Indianapolis, Lenae decides to let curiosity lead. This is her first time this far north, after all. Driessen introduces her to Chef Fiel Bick. He is known all over the world for his chicken noodle soup. Lenae stares at his face, willing herself to remember it. His appearance (as tidy as his restaurant) is as mundane as anything she's seen on a cooking YouTube channel. She looks around his restaurant. The low ceiling is left over from the twentieth century, like Lenae's place, but clearly updated. According to Driessen, this restaurant's fare has been compared to the best historical recreations from the 1930s in New York. Lenae wants to be impressed by Bick, at least for Driessen, but mostly because she wants something outside of her home to impress her. They walk across shining, white-tiled floors to the back room of his tasteful and tidy restaurant.

"I'm sure Rhys told you why he'd bring you to Indianapolis to watch someone make a soup."

"Not really, no." Lenae admits.

"I told her about a helium bath but she's not very interested," Driessen says. They both look at her and chuckle. The humor between them is dry and empty like the old gourds from her great grandmother's kitchen which now hang over her sink. It's unclear if they meant for her to be in on the joke. That part, at least, feels familiar. They make their way to a room in the corner of Bick's immaculate kitchen. From the outside it looks like a sound booth complete with a light above the door. Driessen stands aside while Bick gives Lenae a mask she usually sees on the oldest casino goers.

"Oxygen. When we open the helium bath it quickly boils out. If you were to breathe that much helium at once, it would suck the oxygen out of your system and you'd die." Bick says as he puts the mask over his face, and it instantly suctions on. His breath fogs the clear plastic over his mouth before he presses a vent in front, and it pressurizes. To this point, she'd done her best to indulge her cousin's encouragement to taste a little more life and do it with curiosity instead of judgment. Now, this is officially stupid. She should have never left Louisiana.

"Mr. Bick—"

"Fiel."

"Mr. Bick, I don't think I like any food enough to chance dying over it."

"Perfectly safe, Lenae," Driessen says from behind her.

"Then why don't you have a mask? Why aren't you going in?"

"I only have two masks," Bick informs. "I really only need one. Helium bath is a one-person job. I have that extra just in case." His voice is muffled through the plastic. He can see Lenae has made no move to put her mask on. She raises an eyebrow as he waits for her to do so. "I just came from the doctor this week. Tip top shape. He said my lungs are the best of all," he attempts to reassure.

Both men continue to watch expectantly. "All right," she says. "I'll look. But then it will be time for me to go home."

Inside the odd little room, he closes the door and seals the latch. Lenae sees the same neutral look on Driessen's face through the tiny window of the space door. The room is smaller than the bathroom at Lenae's restaurant and she feels claustrophobic. There are familiar things next to things which aren't. Cooked chicken sits in a large tub near a silver dome. There are noodles, celery, carrots, salt and pepper sitting near a tube of white particles. Lenae almost mistook them for stuffing in the bean bag chairs she jumped on as a child in her grandmother's house. Bick puts his hand on the silver domed lid.

"This is going to change whatever soup you make into a masterpiece people ponder over for the rest of their lives. Think *Mona Lisa.*"

"Gumbo is not soup." Lenae corrects, but Bick seems as if he doesn't hear her or doesn't care. All Lenae can think is this is an overly complicated way to cook country food. Offering only an expectant stare at Bick, she adjusts her oxygen mask. He seems to get she's not impressed. In quick nervous motions, he presses a button on the left of the dome and pressurized air shoots from invisible holes. Another quick movement and he presses a button on the right, near where the bean bag filling is. The small white balls disappear down the tube, into the silver dome. Bick turns back to face her.

"I've made a broth to start my soup. All the regular ingredients, but with much more water. Once I open up the vents around the bath, the liquid helium I've combined with the broth will start to boil violently. Since liquid helium is ultra-cold, it has frozen the broth. It will re-liquefy in all the boiling. Everything will come out silky. The pellets you saw go in—those are zeolites. They become extremely hot when combined with water, sucking up the extra water in the broth during the heat exchange. Right now, the inside of this bath looks and feels like the earth did when it was made: a violent boiling of essence." On cue, the bath behind him begins to vibrate, moan, and growl. Lenae takes half a step back to the door. "It's an extremely fast process. This will be cooked to perfection in about four more minutes, and we can add in the solids. Have to wait just long enough for things to calm down so the solids don't disintegrate."

"Disintegrate?"

"Oh yeah. This thing will liquefy anything. I leave bones in my broth. Gives it extra flavor you couldn't achieve otherwise."

"I love me some bones in my gumbo. But, Mr. Bick, why go to all this trouble? What's wrong with cooking it the old-fashioned way?"

"Nothing," Bick says, eyes cryptic with the mask covering whatever expression his mouth has taken. "My ancestors made something perfect for their time. This is our time now. And if we can make something better, shouldn't we?"

Lenae considers the question. It doesn't feel rhetorical to her, though she is sure Bick meant it that way. She watches as he combines the final ingredients.

"I think I'll let you finish and wait outside. Not used to being in small spaces like this," she says at the door of the chamber.

"Welcome to the Midwest! All we have are small spaces since the Great Migration from the East Coast. I'll bring you a taste once this comes to temperature."

As she exits the chamber, Driessen has a smile—a seemingly genuine one this time.

"Well? Did you get it? Did you see how it just makes everything better? I mean we all know sauces and soups do better once they've sat and the ingredients get locked in. This gives people the second day flavor in minutes. And it's so silky."

Lenae smiles politely, calculating how many plate lunches she'll have to sell to compensate for a hyperloop ticket home. "It's something."

Driessen rambles on about food theory and how they've had it all wrong. He explains how today's chefs picked up where gastronomy left off seven decades ago, giving us "better eating through chemistry." Bick exits his chamber with his mask swinging around his neck and a pure white bowl in his hand. Lenae quickly takes a bite in hopes it would mask her wariness. The flavors are complex as any gumbo or jambalaya her grandmother made. She gets what silky means, the broth sliding down her throat as if something could be more fluid than liquid. It is indeed the best chicken noodle soup she's ever had. Mostly because it's the only chicken noodle soup she's ever had.

After a polite smile and a thank you to Bick, Driessen calls a private car. She's relieved to be going home by familiar transportation: airplane. It's not until they are through the scanners at the airport that he tells her their next destination is Nigeria, not Dallas. Lenae stops near the middle of the automated walkway in the immense airport, wanting to scream. This is kidnapping. He said a couple of stops, but she had no idea he meant the other side of world. Kiki must have been in on this. Kiki knew she always wanted to go to Africa. Lenae is furious and petrified, and giddy with excitement. It's enough excitement to reconsider the dangers. Going to the place of her ancestors, re-connecting the broken lines of culture and food, was something she'd dreamed of after a lifetime of stories. A daydream of walking through markets, tasting flavors simultaneously foreign and familiar, left her believing there is a piece of her there. If only she could find it and replace what was taken from her ancestors, maybe she wouldn't need food to feel like she's enough. She never imagined she'd get there with some stranger, someone not in her family or from her community. Still, he could maroon her. She hopes she'd be more at home in Nigeria than Indianapolis. As the excitement wins out over worst case scenarios, and she gets past being pressganged into her dreams, there's her restaurant and her regulars at home, like Mr. Boudreaux, to consider. That settles it. Not enough of her is ready for this.

"I need to get home to my restaurant Rhys. Maybe we can do this another time."

"I thought you said your cousins could look after it."

"They've never had to open *and* close the restaurant. This has been interesting, but I'm afraid I can't do this right now."

"This will make your food ready for a world debut."

"What if I don't want to?"

The last few whirlwind hours have her reality violently shifting like Bick's space soup. Her small life was enough until everyone started pushing. Driessen looks at her seriously, his blue eyes boring into her, evaluating her. "What has made you and your food so special is how it's been untouched by all the changes we've seen. It's pure. It's beautiful. It makes sense that you wouldn't want to go mess up a good thing. Your food is your connection, your love, for what everyone before you gave to you. It's the history of your survival. It's the culmination of generations of care. You are special, Lenae. If you don't bring this food into the present, if you don't bring all of what this means to you, that love you've been gifted, and obviously perfected, could be lost forever. It's you or no one." No one has ever been able to understand her cooking on this level, even herself. While the words weave into the unseen holes in her heart, the face and the tone giving them to her remain a mystery. It feels like she's falling, unsure of where the ground is. Her heart pounds, pushing the blood of many generations through her veins quickly, giving her whole body the feeling of weightlessness.

SHE HAS HEARD OF A-HOPPERS, and only now learns the "A" stands for atmosphere. Concord jets were reborn through a hypersonic aircraft that can skip along the top of the Earth's stratosphere like a winged stone. A glider rather than a jet, it launches out above the stratosphere via a maglev (like the ones they use on the hyperloops), using its hydrogen thrusters only to get out near space, and then the one or two more times it takes it to find its trajectory to the port. The flight to Abuja lasts only two hours and takes one skip. Lenae is grateful for several reasons. First is the ascent. It is so drastic, so pressurizing, like taking a supersonic elevator up without being able to lock your legs out. Her stomach jostles up to her brain, threatening to make a hasty exit through her mouth. Second is because of the frigid temperature on the interior of the craft. No wet winter in Natchitoches, and no walk-in freezer in Indianapolis, prepared her for the meat locker of the cabin once they crossed through the stratosphere. Third: the skip. Just as her stomach reverses directions as it comes back down from its launch, the thrusters blast, shoving the craft forward, but smashing Lenae into the back of her seat. Fourth is the view. Seeing Earth from here, the bright blues, lush greens, and muted browns, her town and her family might as well be in the next galaxy. Nothing is recognizable from her window at this height. Last is the descent back through the atmosphere. Despite the super light, super hard, super heat-resistant carbon fiber-silica composite shield on its underbelly, the Artic temperature of the interior warms to what feels like a simmering étouffée. To keep the space jet streamlined, there are only two chairs on each row. She tries to find a comfortable way to sit in her tiny seat. Their bodies spill into each other despite the armrest between them. She holds her breath when his body brushes against her to adjust the air above them. Touch is usually reserved for family and regular customers. Even her own touches are few and far between. She sweats through her clothes. Her intake of breath makes her mindful of the room she takes up.

As they get closer to Africa, reality nears her daydream, almost like watching flour and oil slowly make a dark brown roux. Her breath is even and quick. Without ever having the money or resolve for traveling, she'd resigned herself to subscribing to eighteen YouTube channels broadcasted from the continent. The images of smiling people—her people—with their tech advancements, in colorful garments, eating colorful food from colorful bowls, enamored her from the first video years ago.

But a familiar fear of the unfamiliar does find her. Cameras edit out images of the Africa people would rather remain unseen, the same way she polices her social media entries to make sure the pictures of her food look good enough (never mind pictures of her). Watching the Earth speed by at over 300,000 mph leaves her wondering if meeting Africa after YouTube will feel similar to eating Bick's chicken soup. The rest of the country decided that was ultimate comfort food. While delicious, there was no comfort for Lenae in that bowl, not like what she feels with a jambalaya or étouffée. Will Africa be this way? Alterations to her daydream appear. Africa has had at least seven different wars being waged at any given time during the last twenty years. When Driessen made quick mention of Nigeria being the only African country at peace with America during liftoff, it did nothing to calm her nerves. His absence of clear emotional expression while saying it unsettled her more. This trip has given her secrets to the world's recipes, only to find out they are cheats and empty. Stealing the daydream that is her family's continent of origin, and the food within, to make her feel complete, will be too much. As she sits, her stomach forces to her throat while her chest feels it might break the invisible barriers of her seat. Lenae may never be ready to have her understanding of the past be corrupted by the present.

Those feelings render from her like fat from cracklins' after disembarking from the A-hopper. The country is awash in black skin not lightened by four hundred years of colonialization and rape. This pure vision of her unseen, stolen past is beautiful. Questions about her own Blackness, and if she is enough for this place, haunt her. But they are only a faint flavor in light of the beauty. Smiling, beautiful faces sit upon proud shoulders while long strides take these people about their day across the land they were never forced to leave. It's all so unfamiliar. But watching the comfort of people who look like her, and feel at home, rocks her to her core. She cries silently, wiping the tears immediately should they be too much.

From her window in their car, where she can still watch but not be expected to participate, she can see YouTube did none of this justice. People call loudly to one another. They look her in the eye, unapologetically trying to figure her out. There is more color and technology than she can take in. Many wear draping clothes with interfaces built-into the cloth thanks to the graphite microchips the country has produced. This is not the Africa her parents talked about. She wonders if her family would talk with the same pity in their voices if they knew Louisiana has been left behind in the times much more than here. Could this place, which she has no memory of, recognize something familiar in her? Would Africa welcoming back her lost child be enough for her and all her ancestors? Equal parts of amazement and homesickness rumble in her unsettled tummy. She remains in such a trance that Driessen must shake her to call her attention to the sights.

"It's even more crowded than the last time I was here," Driessen says dryly. He is not as hypnotized by throngs of Black people, their easy rhythms of speech, and their movements. Their facial expressions are so loud they make Louisiana feel quiet in comparison. Lenae remembers an episode on YouTube about how everyone in Lagos retreated here to Abuja because of the rising sea, something relatable. Difference and similarity blur together so quickly she feels like an over-stirred sauce piquant. Driessen watches her with a practiced warm smile. The disquiet she's felt at that smile is overpowered by sights and sounds around her. She startles when they arrive at their destination. Driessen must hold her arm as they exit the car because she is looking everywhere except where her feet are going.

"Lenae, meet Chef Thomas Achebe. He is president of the Nigerian Cuisine Association. And he is using the helium bath." Achebe is a lithe man. Despite his dark, good looks, Lenae was taught to never trust a thin chef. But he doesn't look at her like she is used to. Normally men either can't acknowledge her, or their eyes eat at her without ever tasting who she is. His eyes are kind and friendly. They don't hurt her to look at her. Questions about his ability as a chef are swatted away as Achebe's glowing smile appears. It takes a while for her to listen through his accent without getting hypnotized by the rhythm of his speech. She realizes her accent is the foreign one. As he walks her through how he uses the helium bath for Afang soup, she watches with less skepticism than she did with Bick in Indianapolis. This man, with his beautiful skin, and genuine warm smile, could not be a shifty trend bender.

The meal is good, or at least, Lenae assumes so. Like the chicken noodle soup, it's the first she's had. There are flavors her mouth has never experienced and doesn't know what to do with. At least there is crawfish in it to make it familiar. She blames herself for not completely liking it. She catches herself missing her family's famous turkey neck jambalaya. A bout of self-consciousness kicks her in the stomach nearly as violently as the plane ride had. The Afang is complex and pure, not born of generations of toil and survival in a place that only wanted her ancestors' labor. Achebe's food was refined from unbroken generational lines. It never had to stand up for itself, talk back, or subvert its true meaning to continue to exist. And without those things, the Afang doesn't feel like enough. Her stomach settles a little.

This isn't the last time she is disillusioned. She remained mostly silent while Thomas and Driessen chatted during dinner. They did not try to include her, but they also did not exclude her. Achebe smiled at her warmly, appearing completely at home in this restaurant, in this country, and on this continent. His confident, easy way speaks of knowing his history and living in an unbroken line. After the dinner conversation, Achebe offers her a place to stay and to show her around. Lenae's mind swoons while her body and soul sag. She wants to feel at home. She wants Thomas to make her feel at home. But it's not here. A deep desire to accept this invitation from a long-lost brother, cousin, or even lover who has been waiting for her, rumbles next to the Afang upsetting her stomach. It doesn't help that the speed of life in the last twenty-four hours has not been marinated with love and slowly simmered the way she is used to, leaving his invitation feeling as foreign as the spices here. She worries she will never feel the way Achebe feels in his home. Even though her restaurant had been in her family for three generations, and her ancestors were enslaved to her country and continent several generations before, she has never felt comfortable enough. Watching Achebe makes her want to live in her home fully.

With downturned eyes she tells Achebe she has to go back. Driessen's response is his usual practiced smile. Achebe lets her know the offer stands while she walks this earth. She returns the offer, hoping he does not take her up on it. She knows her little life with little technology, in her little, wet corner of the world, cooking from only a few generations worth of memory, and the little bit of culture and love she was left with, could never be enough for a man like him like it is enough for her.

Back on the A-Hopper, Lenae decides she will not pretend any longer for this cryptic man. "Why, Rhys? Why did you spend all this money, bring me across the country, then across the ocean, to see this helium bath thing? What's in this for you?"

"Your company." The suspicion that has simmered throughout this trip boils and she searches his eyes for something, or anything. The blue pool of his eyes, blue as the ocean they speed over, seems empty. They still hold no message, and she wonders how much it would take to fill them. Driessen speaks softly as they watch each other. "I wanted you to see how we think what we have and what we've been taught is enough. But with each other we can be more than enough." Lenae smiles and pushes a few curls from her face. She stops caring about spilling into his seat while their eyes remain locked. Reflected in his blue pools is her image. Normally, reflections are something she'd avoid. These trips have unpacked all the fears and insecurities and left them out where he can see them. Not once has he backed away. The jostling of the plane lands her face close enough to his pointed nose that she can smell the pepper from their dinner on his breath. The plane shakes violently on its skip, enough to send the essence of Nigeria from her gut onto Driessen's tailored shirt.

DRIESSEN DOESN'T MAKE ANY mention of being thrown up on the whole ride from DFW to Natchitoches. In fact, he doesn't talk about much except for what Lenae will need to do to get ready to become an international sensation. Maybe they could start with lab grown meats, just to get people to buy in, he tells her while dabbing at a few remaining vomit spots on his shirt. The thought of mixing meat from a lab with rice from a root is a level of unnatural Lenae can't comprehend. Driessen orders the helium bath right there on the car's touch screen. Lenae doesn't dare object out of embarrassment. It's happening even faster than her world tour, forcing decision-making into a blurred assessment of the moment. Bick and Achebe plan to begin international promotion through travel syndicates in two weeks in hopes the rich food tourists of the world would start A-Hopping into their restaurants. Driessen thinks it will be good to start her promotion alongside them. At least she would not have to ride that damned aircraft to the customers.

"We need to get this helium chamber constructed fast," Driessen says as the car pulls onto her street.

"How fast?"

"Now," Driessen responds looking straight ahead. A con-struction crew with a truckload of materials is in the gravel parking lot of her humble restaurant. "You just need to sign a few things."

She looks up at him, and his blue eyes are still, empty pools. This isn't the way she'd hope to let her family's legacy, Hedricks's Creole and Soul Food, live on in this chang-ing world. But now that she's seen two places outside her hometown, and seen how food is evolving, feeding the Mr. Boudreauxs of Natchitoches (a soon to be washed out town) doesn't seem like enough for her family's legacy—even if it would be enough for her. After she flashes her face as ID for the contract, she looks back up at him. His face is inches from hers again. His lips are smiling. She looks down at them and then back at his blank eyes.

"We're going to make a great team," he says. He exits the car into the drizzle.

WAKING UP AGAIN IN HER HOME, alone, feels different than it did just forty-eight hours ago. She slept for longer than she can ever remember sleeping. It adds to the dreamlike quality of the previous day. She makes herself strong synthetic coffee and heads for her restaurant. The morning solitude and the routine almost make her forget what she agreed to last night. Waiting for her is a half complete helium chamber with a newly installed helium bath. She knows she should set about starting the day's special, but all she can do is sit at the table farthest from her nearly demolished kitchen and stare at the silver dome. Like the trip to Africa, she hadn't really considered what this would be like. And like Afang and chicken-noodle soup, it's nothing as advertised. She continues to stare until long after her strong syn coffee is gone and Driessen has arrived.

"The crew isn't here?" he asks when he walks in. Lenae still gazes at the corner. When she looks up, it's not at him, but at her grandmother's handwriting on the menu chalkboard. It's harder to see now with a layer of construction dust. She spies her gumbo pot on a magnet burner. Someone left their nail gun inside of it, the hydraulic canister poking out of top. Her life, her food, her memory, and her love are all shifting. When she does look at Driessen, his lips smile but his eyes don't twinkle—or dart—still making it impossible to know what the man is feeling. Much more clearly now, she remembers the way she was reflected in his eyes. The bottomless blue held her image there. Her reflection looked as if it could drown in them. With a night of sleep in her, her perspective isn't as fuzzy. Maybe she thought she could drown in those eyes because there was nothing there to hold onto.

Over the helium bath in Indianapolis, she felt like her food wasn't enough. Then in Nigeria, she did not feel like she—herself—was enough of anything. But this restaurant and this food were built from lifetimes of real sacrifice and heavy work. It's late nights cleaning up and singing with her mother. It's working the line with Daddy. It's Granny CeCe's shoulder aching from nonstop stirring of roux. It's whispered recipes never written. Her family's food and the restaurant's reputation have been earned. And then it was all entrusted to her. They thought she was enough. She trusts them. Their love and trust are not as empty and fast as liquefied air. Another look at the ghost of her grandmother's handwriting on the board and Lenae decides living a life heavy with work, love, trust, and survival, is more than enough.

"I can't do this," Lenae says. The corner of Driessen's lips drop.

"You've just got nerves again. They will pass, I promise."

Looking back to the nail gun in the gumbo pot, Lenae shakes her head and her thick curls bounce heavily.

Driessen steps closer. "This will be a catalyst of the meat return. If we're not fast enough, we'll miss our chance. Food trends flash and burn."

"You're doing all of this because of a food trend you want to be a part of?"

"*We* are. Yes," he says while passing a pointing finger between the two of them.

"And what happens to *me* when the food trend is over? What happens to *my* restaurant, *my* family's cooking, and *my* life when *my* food isn't trending?"

"We have time to figure that out."

Lenae guffaws. "Not enough time, Mr. Driessen."

"What are you saying?"

"I'm saying take all this shit and get out."

"You signed contracts yesterday. You'll owe me a lot of money if you back out now."

Lenae gets up and walks past him into the kitchen, glancing again at her grandmother's dust-covered handwriting. There's no need to worry about what he will think or what they will say. She's had enough. Grabbing her favorite cleaver, she walks back to the dining room wordlessly, with a dangerous sway to her hips. She sees his bland eyes questioning her intentions. When those flavorless eyes come up to meet hers, and he sees the gusto and spice invented and refined by her ancestors, he backs out the door. She watches him peel out of the driveway, cleaver still in hand.

Turning back to the chalkboard, tears find her. She slumps to the floor and drops the cleaver. She almost does not notice the door opening behind her. Kiki wraps her arms around her cousin without speaking. They sit together on the floor, quietly rocking back and forth, until Kiki sees the helium bath in the corner.

"What the fuck is that?"

"Girl, I don't even know where to start."

Kiki opens one of the compartments on her bright turquoise waterproof shirt and hands Lenae a nebulizer pen. "That's got the good stuff, that 'Soak' shit. You take a big hit and tell Kiki all about it."

Lenae tells her about Indianapolis and Fiel Bick, the helium bath, the backwards soup, and the petrifying A-hopper rides. She turns on the helium bath and opens the lid to display its absurdity. Kiki's eyes light up as Lenae describes a high-tech Nigeria. Lenae can see her planning a trip as they talk about thin, quiet Thomas Achebe, his confusing Afang, intoxicating voice, perfect smile, and his open invitation. What Lenae can't tell is if her cousin would want Thomas for Lenae or herself. Lenae has run out of energy to tell her cousin she absolutely cannot do the unfamiliar anymore. As if Kiki can sense this, she tells Lenae what she saw in the parking lot.

"So, I guess with Driessen taking off like that you're done with him."

"Kiki, I—"

"I didn't like him anyway. Wasn't no soul to him, even for a white boy." Kiki's voice goes up at the end, sounding cartoonish. They both look over at the helium bath and see it still on and open. Between the lessened oxygen, and the weed, the two fall out laughing. The squeaky laughs lead to hysterics, chasing away any tears left for Driessen and his plans. "But that Boudreaux out there, Lord." Kiki squeaks between laughs.

"What are you talking about?" Lenae peeps back.

"Looked like I ran over that man's puppy when I told him you weren't here yesterday. He picked at that turkey neck jambalaya. Didn't put down the whole plate like he normally do." Kiki giggles at her own voice.

"Kiki, that ain't funny."

"Then you should tell him that. He's been in the parking lot since before I pulled up. He probably seen old white boy rollin' gravel."

Lenae stands and peeks out the window. Sure enough, Boudreaux's waiting patiently in his car. His dark brown eyes twinkle brightly when he sees Lenae. He smiles contently like it's enough.

Bone to Pick

There must be a better way to rig this trap, and since Osmin is involved, there is. His thick fingers work the nylon rope expertly, making a noose where there would normally be a hook. Sweat pours through his wicking shirt as he hangs the trap from the tree. Around errant branches, he loops the noose to keep it open. The bait dangles from its own noose above the bigger one. The gator will have to go through the big noose, and when it yanks the bait, that bigger noose would close around its thick body. He'd raised the complaint of how archaic the hooks are, usually injuring or even killing the specimens Wildlife and Fisheries is trying to save. But he was told no one had ever found a better way. Most likely because no one tried, he decides.

He could have been an engineer like his two brothers. His doctor and nurse sisters saw his affinity for biology and thought he should be in the medical field. Osmin's curiosity was about the imperative of evolution. Whereas his brothers and sisters trust people and things, Osmin trusts only nature. And with four older siblings making so much money to take care of their mother, he can trust their attachment to their parent so he can help Mother Earth survive without guilt weighing him down.

Osmin squints against the glare of the water, his office. Previously, Lake Martin was his playground after his family relocated from New Orleans when he was a child. It was natural to make water his workplace. It's not like he had a choice when the Henderson Swamp, pregnant with runoff from big storms in the north, and water creeping from the Gulf, expanded to claim the lake. Remaining feels like a family tradition. His family held onto the jungles and fields of Honduras long after they were fruitful. It wasn't until years of drought, coupled with the rising sea, forced them away. Abuelo sent Osmin's mother away, only a child then, during the droughts of 2018. His grandfather elected to stay behind, and Osmin's mother could never decide if it was because of hope or nostalgia. COVID-19 found Abuelo in late 2020. His mother would laugh at how she left not enough water for too much. She also laughs at how much Osmin is like the grandfather he never met. Osmin lingers in the past. But none of the subsequent viruses have come for him. Osmin likes to think no new pandemics have gotten a foothold in Louisiana because even old death thawed from permafrost respects life that's thrived in his region since the last ice age.

He rounds the point of one of the many shifting, floating islands in the swamps on the mainland side of the levee sea wall. He smells a couple of men fishing out of an old first gen hybrid boat. No matter how many regulations they put on petroleum, the people in this state can't seem to break their longing for crude—or is it crudeness. It's almost as bad as their addiction to plastic or their scant regulation on farming. He approaches the fishing boat at an idle. Both men are drenched from the drizzle and humidity. They look sheepish as they reel their lines up to show they have nothing on them.

"Y'all catching?" asks Osmin.

"Not a bite. Same as usual."

"Can I check your well?"

Both men eye each other and Osmin. They would have complied instantly if he had lighter skin and hair. The water and land can change, but some things don't. It probably doesn't help that he is younger than both of them by ten years. They look around forty.

"Sure," says the younger looking of the two white men, succumbing to the affable grin Osmin keeps on his visage. His wide mouth is always perched in preparation for a cynical laugh.

"Move to the bow, please," Osmin instructs, not needing the boat terminology. He does it to sound more important and authoritative.

He checks their livewell, and it is indeed empty. There are no lines over the side of the boat, hiding fish in the water. He's learned, though, to always check the beer cooler. There he finds a small alligator gar. These are the most abundant fish found in these waters lately, and therefore have few restrictions on them. He looks up at the two men who are still wincing from when he opened the cooler. This ugly dinosaur of a fish isn't worth eating, and this particular one is too small to sell as a trophy to the new breed of hoarders in this country: Animal Enthusiasts. Enthusiasts are modern day pirates. Trying to steal pieces of life, they end up robbing the future. Like Osmin, they see wildlife as the earth's vanishing art. The difference is they want to own it while Osmin just wants to participate in it. It's people like them Osmin tolerates the least.

Running his fingers over the bony plates of the gar, he thinks about how Enthusiasts would be his ticket to doing what is needed for Mother Earth if they didn't destroy every-thing they touch. Enthusiasts counted all the megafauna out, their extinction so imminent that the difference between living specimen and fossil is a short enough time we might as well speed it along. If the extinction tourism companies (who give higher prices for critically endangered species) weren't so morally repugnant, he would be making more money than any of his siblings. With that kind of money, he would start his nonprofit to force humans into divesting themselves completely from the natural environment. A nuclear melt-down at Chernobyl did that, keeping the humans out. Life returned, albeit somewhat mutated. The takhi was the last wild breed of horse and fared better against radiation than against humans. Maybe Osmin could do the reverse and get humans to stay in their cities, to inhabit human-only spaces, so the rest of the world could heal from our ignorance. He looks up at these two poachers, smiling accusingly, thinking how they'd be some of the first he'd move out of these wet-lands into concrete cages of urban apartments where they couldn't ignorantly hurt Earth any longer. But ignorance is only part of what make poachers collect bits of struggling life in this part of the world. These two fishermen are likely keeping this animal out of habit since Louisianans believe sport-fishing is an identity. It's enough to make Osmin feel pity. He, too, isn't sure if he remains here, doing what he does, out of habit or identity.

Osmin rubs his damp, sweating, buzz-cut head. "I'll let y'all keep this one," he says with an air of grandeur, his wide mouth smiling.

Back on his boat, waving with sarcastic cheer to the fisher-man as he pulls away, he turns a corner down a narrow bayou and stops. Before him is an opening into a floating island. At first, he thinks it's the nice healer lady's place, the one that treated his warts several years ago. Except that freaky island is on the other side of the levee wall. It would be so much easier to send the drone over the area, but he never trusts its readings or its camera. Satellite photos would be even more useless. Nothing can compare with using one's own body, the one nature gave to us, to interact with the world. Eventually, he recognizes it as a location where he left a surveillance box for poachers alongside a trap. He placed them there because of the tail drag marks around a shallow pond on the interior of the floating mass. Wading into the murky water will be relief from this heat. He passes an uncertain hand again through the black stubble atop his head.

His electric outboard has an extendable Go-Devil prop, and he lets it drop only a few inches under the water's surface. A cool mist floats on the water in the cove. Chinese Tallow branches reach for him. Somehow, they've managed to figure out the water without needing a tap root buried deep, piquing Osmin's admiration. Osmin feels his shoulders finally let go of the disrespect the two fishermen showed their Mother. He shivers from the effect. He immediately shivers again, this time at the sight of a white belly on the far bank of the shallow pond.

Poachers removed the head, feet, and tail of an eight-foot gator. Those will fetch a handsome price from Enthusiasts. It's big enough they decided to strip the parts rather than lug the body. In fact, it's the biggest Osmin has seen in over a year, though the last one was alive. The poachers didn't even bother to keep the skin and meat like the old Cajuns would. This is a middle finger to the Conservationists. Osmin looks up at his camera, carefully hidden in the thick growth surrounding the pond. It should have notified the central office of any movement. It is untouched. Someone electronically sabotaged it. *All the tech in the world won't save these people. It's just another way to destroy themselves,* he thinks.

The emotionlessness of the dispatcher as Osmin calls in the poach's GPS coordinates is disheartening. It sounds like resignation. He knows there's no way to track these moving islands, but no one here wants to fight anymore. Between the lack of interest from his team and the work entailed to move the heavy beast onto the boat (without the help of a winch), Osmin decides to do a field necropsy rather than bring it into the lab. They probably won't be thorough enough to learn more about, or from, a creature which will outlast everything. Lowering his stocky frame onto the narrow slip of mud by the water, he straddles the carcass. From the looks of the blood, and the lack of decomposition, this likely happened either last night or the night before. He pulls his Bowie knife from his boot, the ten-inch broad blade glinting in the dim sunlight—a tool time tested and adaptable. He opens the body cavity.

A moment is spent in ritual respect for the alligator heart. Four chambered like ours, but with the Foramen of Panizza allowing oxygenated blood to mix with non-oxygenated blood, making it perfect for deep diving. Only whales have a more efficient heart. They also have those amazing brains. In training off the coast, Osmin had another moment of respect when extracting organ samples from a wayward orca who'd washed up. Their limbic systems are far more advanced than humans', making them much more capable to feel emotions even humans can't. As Osmin explores the cavity of this alligator for life history clues, he continues to wonder when the Anthropocene will end so a new creature can close the gap between surviving and feeling.

He finds nothing notable in the lungs or reproductive system of the alligator. This creature, surpassing the four-foot requirement for survival, except against the deadliest predators—humans—was healthy and would have likely created many more viable specimens of its kind. Osmin opens the gator's stomach. Hooks, bits of plastic, and fish bones are abundant. There is something else, something very different, amongst the detritus. The largest intact object is a porous, fibrous, almost comb-like spoon shaped apparatus. It's as long as his Bowie knife, nearly a foot in length. Osmin first thinks the incredibly acidic gator stomach somehow merged a plastic brush with a bird's skull. But after cleaning it off he sees the two are very clearly attached and all part of the same skull. This creature is completely unknown to Osmin, whose knowledge of the fauna here is encyclopedic. He sets it aside to complete his field necropsy. Denying child-like hope, he tries to ignore what this could mean. As he notates observations and measurements on the interface embedded in the arm of his green coveralls, his eyes are constantly drawn back to the alien skull. Picking it back up, he falls into the wonder which brought him to this job in the first place.

Could this be a new species? If it is, it will alight the world. Osmin contains the skull within a sterile plastic baggie before containing the excitement beginning to show in his heart rate. Childhood wonder, originally sparked when his mother would tell of prolific wildlife present before she was forced out of Honduras by the climate, floods his chest. Osmin would search the waterways and foliage of Louisiana for the same sort of biodiversity, only to watch it wane throughout his thirty years. He's ached for proof that Mother Earth may not have shown all her tricks yet.

Despite tempered enthusiasm, he pushes his boat to its fastest speed, racing to bring the skull back to Central. It's several minutes before he can get into the lab because the techs want him decontaminated. He's unable to convey his urgency to get the DNA of this specimen decoded because he's being sprayed down with disinfectant and air dried. The skull is decontaminated without the same interest Osmin shows in it. The six scientists in the room just managed to produce viable speckled trout embryos and didn't want their work undone. In fact, he must call one of the biologists away from his screens, set on algae blooms being bioengineered to increase their carbon capture, to have a look at a natural specimen. The biologist disinterestedly explains this is not a skull and likely some partially digested hard plastic.

Looking at the natural specimen in his right hand and his small field interface screen with the pictures and measurements of the dissected alligator still pulled up on his left arm, Osmin fumes. The scientists are so set on trying to hold on to the life they've known, to stop losing, they can't appreciate for one second how this could be a way forward. Osmin ponders why humans can't see loss as a part of evolving. When an organism no longer needs an aspect of their anatomy, it is lost. Lose a job, lose a relationship, lose a way of thinking, being, and doing—and gain life. Osmin figures our extinction is happening because we won't let ourselves lose and be reborn through the reckless and merciless, yet fair, womb of Mother Earth. Mother Earth no longer needs humans to try and save her. She needs us to get out of her way. The bone in his hand is made of unfettered promise—more than these manufactured fish eggs in plastic tanks, surrounded by sensors, microscopes, and computer interfaces. His wide, perpetual smile curves downward in disgust. If they can't even lose naturally, he will help them. He stabs his bowie knife through the nearest server and launches it into a bank of screens, which then topples into a case of artificial eggs containing the speckled trout embryos.

Over the hum of his hybrid outboard motor, the screams of the biologists echoing pleasantly in his ears, he thinks of where to go to get a better idea of what this creature is. He turns the light, airy skull in his hands while considering. Nearly all the fishermen around here are leery of him. The Federal Wildlife Association wouldn't cooperate since he just destroyed thousands of dollars of equipment and set their research back by at least a year. More local knowledge is what's needed.

Arlis is a nice guy despite his lack of expression and misplaced faith in humanity. He caresses the skull in his hands and says he's never seen anything like it in his years in either the Coast Guard or the Cajun Navy. But there is a man who would know. Arlis tells Osmin about old Mr. Hebert in the islands past the levee wall. Arlis's new girlfriend, who turns out to be the faith healing lady, arrives with groceries.

"How's those warts?" she asks loudly. Osmin looks at Arlis and flushes.

"You should hear the medical issues of mine she talks about in mixed company," Arlis says to Osmin while looking at his girlfriend. His normally blank face is filled with love. It's a different kind of love than Osmin has seen between most humans. Arlis has slimmed since they got together. His smile is peaceful, elated in expectancy, while helping his partner unpack the groceries. Hers is one a goddess might show her worshipper, though she doesn't seem interested in commanding. They have something much of the human species can't seem to figure out. We would be this attuned to each other, Osmin laments, if we still lived in our small family groups as we were evolved to do. This is the reason the dog is the only creature Osmin does not respect. We selfishly perverted nature by bioengineering wolves just so we wouldn't be lonely. Declining a dinner invitation from Sarah and Arlis due to excitement about the skull, felt against the backdrop of unexpected jealousy, he turns his boat toward the GPS coordinates Arlis gives him. He makes sure to use his personal GPS so the lab won't track him.

His round hull boat struggles against the wake of the fishing vessels amongst the mangroves. The lack of life in the water only makes them fish harder, like an addict running out of his drug. Osmin grumbles audibly, hoping the fishermen will be some of the first to go when Mother Earth returns us to her measured chaos. When She does, he knows what it will mean for humans. We will have to get smaller. The dinosaurs shrank to birds once Earth was done with their dominance. Giant ground sloths stood twelve feet tall thousands of years ago and are now no bigger than teddy bears. Shrinking will mean we continue to exist. Could losing our perceived dominion result in the shrinking of our brains, possibly limiting logical thought and self-awareness? This makes Osmin's smiling countenance widen. What wins in our wasteland and dominates the next will participate in the rules of Nature. *Then we could be domesticated, made to work like the beasts of burden we've subjugated in our history*, he thinks. At least this dominion would be more egalitarian across our species than humans' record of enslaving only certain members of our own kind. He's left with the image of saddled horses following the breaking of their spirit. We might even thank our masters for domesticating us since it prevents our extinction. It's hard to say what we'd value more: freedom or our lives. In school, Osmin learned Americans always value freedom more. But unlike a war of ideals, one thankfully not fought in four generations, there will be no winner or loser; only those species that survive and those that don't.

Atop two flights of stairs to Mr. Hebert's house, there is a new hard plastic porch. Mr. Hebert sits at attention in his wheelchair on an uncovered piece of deck amidst the spray and drizzle as if he is waiting for someone. An old-style steel colored rain jacket is thrown carelessly over his head and shoulders, the front agape while the back drapes over the wheelchair battery. Mr. Hebert greets him and has synthetic coffee in his hand before Osmin can state the purpose of his visit. Mr. Hebert begins telling stories before Osmin can say anything.

"Poo yie but dis rain!"

"Back in '25, Pilar washed dis house ten miles away and…"

"My wife, she was da best cook. She could make jambalaya, fry up fish…"

It takes everything for Osmin to refrain from cutting off this elder and his inane babbling as he nervously turns the skull in his hands. Finally, a pause between topics is big enough to reveal the skull and ask about the fate of all living things. Mr. Hebert turns the skull over in his leathery hands, pulling it back and forth in front of his cloudy eyes, his bushy brows pumping up and down as if they are trying to well a memory from deep in his mind.

"Paddlefish," he exclaims, toothlessly smiling at his recognition. Punctuating his declaration, the sun emerges from behind its near perpetual cloud cover.

"What's that?"

"Old, old fish. Came from way before da dinosaurs. You'd find dem in rivers and swamps. Dey eat little stuff by keeping deir big mouths open all day." Hebert holds the skull to his nose and opens his gummy mouth wide underneath it. Paired with the slick skin of his raincoat, the old man's impression is a clear picture of what this ugly creature looked like. Osmin is disgusted by the sight, much more than if it were the fish itself. If it weren't for the fact this leftover is a fossil in his own right, refusing even cheap dental implants, he might have educated the man on how disrespectful he is to timeless Nature.

"Are you sure?"

"No," said Hebert, almost happily. "We never got down to da skull when my daddy caught one. We just fried dat up. Pretty good eating."

"I read about paddlefish. They weren't sustainable. Last known specimen died in 2041."

"Maybe not," Hebert says, tossing the skull back to him. Osmin's whole body tenses as he catches the delicate bone before it flies over his shoulder and down twenty feet back into the water. The old man's carelessness, coupled with his morbidly jovial attitude about seeing a fish he thought dead since his youth, is almost more than Osmin can handle. The old timer's nonchalance merges with the destruction of a lifetime of hope. His wide smile reduces to a thin, pursed line as he eyes the skull in his hand. Fury peppers Osmin's face. He stood on the precipice of Mother Earth's salvation, of pure forward movement last seen in this old man's childhood, only to have it severed off with no ceremony or respect—like the head, feet and tail of a poached alligator—leaving only an empty, decomposing heart.

"But hang onto dat. Dat's special. He din't make it dis far on wishes and prayers. He… how you say dat…sustained, even dough he shouldn't have," Hebert says.

Osmin brings his dark eyes, ringed in livid bloodshot, to meet the cloudy ones of Mr. Hebert. Osmin's hands, wrinkled by moisture, turn the skull over, desperately running his fingers over the rough ladle-shaped paddle. There is no promise that we will figure out how to lose in order to live. Osmin feels smaller. Should he decide to yoke another generation with the burden of surviving, the story of this skull will be as much a fairy tale to Osmin's offspring as his mother's lived history was to him. His eyes mist at the thought that his mother went through all this, migrated to find a viable environment for her and her offspring, only for him to fail. This is a good time to leave. He's sure his grandfather would have agreed. Migrating species tend to fare better in volatile environments than ones that settle. They become better equipped to cooperate and coexist. He clearly isn't ready for those things. Not now. Because of his actions earlier in the day his job is dead, his reputation is extinct, and with this specimen turning out to be nearly a fossil, he has lost any chance of surviving here. Does that meanevolution can happen then? Since he (a human) lost, does the earth have a chance to live and grow? Does he?

Osmin passes his hand over his short hair. He is back to feeling alone, back to helplessly watching Mother fade away. He looks up at Mr. Hebert. The momentary sunlight brightening the empty space between the two men retreats again behind a cloud. It starts to rain. The old man watches him, a compassionate look on his face. The look slows Osmin's breathing. How can he know Osmin's angst? How did Mr. Hebert even make it here? Despite all their losses, the old ones, like this old fossil of a man sitting on a sliver of land bordering the sea, are still here, sustaining and possibly thriving. Osmin remembers cases of isolated species, often living at the edges of a population, that "jump" forward in evolution while the rest of the life crumbles. Mother has always carefully selected Her survivors to birth into the next stage of evolution. Osmin considers that it's him that hasn't respected Nature's wisdom enough. His dream needs to evolve. It's enough to make Osmin want to call his siblings and visit his mother.

"He did what da best of us can do," Mr. Hebert says against the hiss of water from above and below.

Shelter in Place

Dung places the jade bracelet in the velvet jewelry bag, and then the bag into her pocket. She does not have the silk bag her mother kept it in, and the guilt from its absence creeps into her heart. She feels its weight heavy against her leg. She imagines, for a moment, that it could anchor her to this spot and she would not have to leave again.

Having to choose what things to leave behind and which to take before a Category 6 hurricane is torture. Having to do it twice in one lifetime is cruel. Dung feels like she's always done it and will always have to do it. When her grandparents left Vietnam by boat in 1978, they'd had far worse choices. Dung reminds herself of this as she watches her daughter, Amelia, pack her brother Amon's truck. Hurricane Pilar did not allow Dung the luxury of getting all her family out fifty years ago. Not a tear is shed as she recognizes this storm will take one of the few things she has left at almost sixty years old: history. She unconsciously rubs the interwoven tattoos of Vietnam and an outline of Orleans Parish on her shoulder, the color and texture of the ink having lessened with time. But she absolutely does not cry. She looks up at the sky, currently sunny with just a few breezy clouds, and thinks she doesn't have it in her to call another place home.

When she looks back down the street at the frantic packing of her neighbors, teeming little ants swarming in and out of their hills, she wishes she would have gotten to know them better. In New Orleans East, she'd known everyone for several blocks. They all shared food, songs, and Sunday evenings. It didn't matter if they were kin because living in New Orleans meant the city was your family. After Pilar blew that home away, Dung lost some of the energy needed to create a community and regrets it most now.

One house has no ants swarming. The lady in the big house—Jennifer, she thinks her name is—doesn't even have a car in the driveway. Dung brought food to Jennifer once or twice, a gesture of respect for an elder. She figured the lonely woman must be in her mid-eighties. They'd shared synthetic coffee and painful silence. Dung decides she at least deserves to have someone check to make sure she's left. Amelia and Amon will wait for her. Taking Dung away from the spinning storm in the gulf is why they'd come here after all.

Dung knocks and waits. She knocks again. Her urge to check on the lonely old white lady, and perhaps a desire to postpone leaving for just a bit longer, compels her to try the door. It opens and she bows her head in, calling Jennifer's name, hoping she remembered it right. The prominent security system watches her on the porch. When there is no answer, she walks inside to see a perfectly clean house. Dung is a little surprised, seeing as how white women don't *need* to keep their houses clean. No dust lay on the ornate hutches. Everything seems to have a place. The dining room table near the entry way has silverware set out as if company is arriving. In the kitchen she calls again. An answer finds her from a back room.

"Who is that?"

"Dung Nguyen. I am your neighbor from down the street. I want to see if you have everything you need to leave."

Jennifer appears from behind a door with arms full of frozen meat and a real tiara on her head. Behind a T-shirt of an obscure punk electronic band from the mid-century, Dung can see partially concealed tattoos on the eighty-something woman. Beneath the meat pile are ripped, real cotton jeans. Her pale and heavily wrinkled skin covers a thin frame. Jennifer's hazel eyes have lost none of their sharpness in age as they pierce through Dung.

"Oh, I'm not leaving, honey. Y'all need some meat? Oh. I'm sorry. I didn't even ask if you were vegan or vegetarian."

Ignoring the fact that she'd brought both meat and non-meat dishes to Jennifer the first time she visited, and then remembered to bring only meat dishes on her subsequent visit, Dung responds, "Thank you. We can take the beef."

"There's more in the freezer if you want it. Since it's so hard to come by, no sense in it going to waste …what'd you say your name was again?"

Dung smiles through a wince. "Dung Nguyen."

"Dung. Dung. Dung," Jennifer repeats. She pushes the "y" sound at the beginning too hard before her lips curl firmly around the "u" in the middle and hum at the end. Dung has gotten used to how white English miss the subtle accentuations. It confuses her since English is her native language as well. Anglophones, even in this globalized culture, miss important things in a one syllable word.

"Well, Dung, you're welcome to anything you want. And I do mean anything." Dung wouldn't mind the right to have her name spoken correctly without having to write it out phonetically.

"Why aren't you leaving?" She inspects the old woman more closely. Her take-no-shit attitude leaves an impression that she inhabits her own world fully and everyone else is just visiting. When white people exhibit these behaviors, she either calls them out on their colonizing attitude or avoids them altogether, saving her energy. Between tomorrow being the end of the world, and Jennifer's betrayal of many other American social rules Dung had come to loathe, Dung is intrigued. She wants to know how a woman at this stage of life can act like she has more life in front of her than behind her.

"This damn water, this weather, is done stealing everything from me. This storm wants to take some more. But I'll give away more than it can take. What's left, it can take over my dead body. Tell everybody else on the street to come get what they want before they take off."

Dung is silent as Jennifer continues unpacking the freezer. This decision appears conscious and deliberate. Jennifer has almost thirty years on Dung and an even better memory of Pilar. The storm approaching is bigger, stretching the Category 6 192 mph classification. While the gulf is further from this home in Alexandria, much more so than it was to New Orleans when Pilar hit, she knows what a storm this powerful can do. Jennifer should remember how Pilar redesigned the state. The wall along the Gulf will do little to stop the surge, much less two hundred mile-an-hour winds.

"You must leave," Dung declares. "Come with us. We can make some room for you in our truck."

Jennifer walks back in the room with an armful of frozen sausage this time. She drops them like bricks on the kitchen counter and lets out a long breath. She looks deep into the pile of coiled, frozen meat. Her shoulders droop and her years rush up to find her.

"Pilar took my past. My pictures all molded and were unsalvageable. The hard drives we'd kept the records on were in Baton Rouge in a safe deposit box. They're marsh gravel now. My husband already had bad lungs. The moisture, the constant low-pressure systems, finally stole the rest of his air. The water washed the industry from this place, and my kids had to leave to find jobs."

"We can drive you to your kids."

"No. Not this time. I'm not letting them pick up where the weather left off. I know I only have a little time left. I want it to belong to me. Today I'm choosing how to give my life away rather than rent it to the weather anymore. Besides, I told my kids I wouldn't e-sign the will unless there was a hurricane in my yard knocking on my door. That shut them up." She looks up at Dung now, the past framing her eyes fading. A happy, content smile, one that has much more satisfaction than Dung has ever seen on a living person, finds her face. Jennifer's shoulders square again, and she picks up two packs of the sausage. "You like pork or beef, honey? You chose beef earlier. Oh here, just take both."

When Dung returns to the truck, her children look at the pile of vacuum sealed meat in her hands questioningly but remain silent. They unceremoniously climb into the truck, hit a few icons on the touchscreen, and the truck quickly backs out. Dung can't shake the look of Jennifer's house, her attitude, but most of all, her smile. Dung has never smiled that way. Neither did her mother. The only time she'd seen that smile on someone in her family was on her grandmother when she was child in Vietnam. A grainy photograph, one of the few to make the abrupt trip in 1978, shows a little girl who shared the ownership of her life with the people around her; a little girl whose parents had just enough means to shield her from famine, but not from war. Dung pulls that laminated photograph from its snug resting place, near the velvet bag and jade bracelet, to look at it. Dung's chin is not as small as her grandmother's, though their ears are both small. Dung's hair thins like her grandmother's did before she passed, though Dung has worked hard to keep it in style, a shorter bob currently. This is where their resemblance ends. The smile on her grandmother's young face shines of never having to leave anything or anyone. That smile, one Dung never got to see in life, lacks three generations of running, of guilt, of leaving behind everything and everyone beloved each time. Countenances teetering between determination and resignation populate the pictures in the subsequent years. These were Dung's faces of love. Work is all the faces could see because it alone held hope. Baptized by the fire of undying labor, eventually the family could smile like their ancestors. Until then, all must work, for it too facilitated the running. At least it was a hopeful run. Working and running embedded themselves so deeply into the family they are now instincts.

Dung looks to her children across the cab. Their young faces stare out of the windows, set with the same resolve of her parents when they moved Dung away from New Orleans. It catches her breath in her throat. Her kids are ready to run to Dallas and get back to work. Amelia and Amon don't deserve to have this be their heritage and legacy. The world's weather makes refugees of everyone by shrinking safe places. Running will not be useful soon. Eventually, there will be nothing to work on or towards. Amon and Amelia will never understand this because they've been born to family, born to a world, which tells them they must run and work. Dung's eyes sting and she blinks away the threat of tears. *I can cry in my grave,* she thinks. All the work has been for this. The running must stop here. Because we are only working toward, and running to, our graves.

"Let me out."

"Are you sick?" Amon asks frustratedly.

"No."

"We can't go back for something. The storm will be here tomorrow morning and the traffic app can't keep up with the evacuation contraflow. We'll get rerouted through Arkansas or something."

"I'm staying."

"What?"

Both now eye her seriously from their seats across the truck cabin. Dung commands the truck to stop, angry resolve rimming her voice. When she exits, Amon and Amelia do as well, faces still resolute. Instinctively, Dung's face mirrors theirs. Quickly, she remembers her purpose and begins to smile. Amon and Amelia look at each other, not sure what's happening.

"I've loved you both. Like a mother should, but not like I would have wanted to love. You've both turned out to be… You've made me very proud." Her children's faces tense to hold back their tears. "You can cry. It's ok." The siblings look at each other again, still unsure of how to handle this. Dung looks up the street to Jennifer's house and smiles. "I can't leave anymore."

"Mom—"

Dung holds up her hand without looking at Amon. He silences out of respect, but Dung can feel the panic rising in him and Amelia. "When you leave, don't go away from here. Go *to* your homes. When you unpack the truck, keep only things you *want*." Dung opens the back door of the truck and pulls out the frozen meat. "I'm keeping this though."

"Mom—"

Dung no longer has a free hand to silence Amelia. Instead, she smiles warmly. This works the same as a raised hand. "Go home," she tells them. She turns and walks toward Jennifer's old house.

She finds her elder in the backyard starting the outdoor infrared grill. Jennifer exchanged her punk garbs for an elegant white sequined evening dress, matching the white hair where her tiara still perches. The wind is beginning to whip up, blowing around the azaleas and palms, along with Jennifer's dress, revealing more colorful tattoos on her legs. Dung smiles as she places her pile of meat next to one Jennifer has made.

"Thought you were leaving."

"Not anymore," Dung says. "What can I do to help?"

"You're gonna have to help me eat all of this, for starts. There's a shit ton of liquor and wine in the house. Time to start on that."

In the haste to leave New Orleans when she was six, she did not get to experience the hurricane party. In every dodged hurricane since, she'd focused on evacuating. Even when she'd return from the false alarms, she'd leave the emergency bags packed and the supplies stocked. Drinking, cooking feasts, and partying as the world threatens to end is the exact opposite of what her nervous system is trained to do. As she mixes a strawberry daiquiri, the weather report's three-dimensional red image of Hurricane Yara, projected onto the wall behind Jennifer, swirls only slightly slower than her drink in the blender. The anticipated landfall is just a few dozen miles south of this place. Watching its course and speed she downs the daquiri. She mixes another before Jennifer can finish her first.

"Slow down, girl! Damn! You ain't gonna last the night this way."

"Sorry. Never been through a hurricane before."

"How long have you lived here?" Again, Dung winces. Is she asking if she is "American," or is this just another example of how invisible Dung has been to her? Either way, it's not good. She second-guesses if she should have given up family and certainty to stand ground with a stranger.

"Long time," is all Dung uses to describe almost forty years on this street.

"Here. Try this instead." Jennifer hands her a dab pen. "Got it loaded with some excellent local stuff. Not that crap corporate brand."

Dung eyes the pen cautiously. Despite marijuana being legal for several decades, this is another new thing. If the weatherwoman is right, she, and everything along the coast of Louisiana, will be washed away by tomorrow afternoon. What has she got to lose? Mimicking the button press and deep inhale she'd watched the neighbors' kids do (but definitely not her kids), she manages to get some pungent vapor from the dab pen. The THC in her veins slows her body enough for her mind to perceive and reflect. As her heart rate drops, she can feel the breeze pushing non-threatening clouds. It's downright pleasant, especially for a late afternoon in August. She smiles as the breeze licks at her sweating forehead and wonders how it can be constantly moving but still balmy. *This breeze isn't happening because I'm running*, she thinks. *This is the breath of the world finding me. While it is fierce and hot, it is not hell.*

"Dung," Jennifer mispronounces, "help me bring these steaks and sausage inside." She hefts a platter of singed meat, too much for any two humans to consume, and follows her hostess inside to the perfectly set dining room table she saw only an hour before. It feels like a day has passed since she rerouted the course of her life.

"Now," Jennifer declares, "grab one of those calligraphy pens on the bureau and hand it to me. It's not a proper feast without names on our settings. How do you spell your name?" she asks while wiggling the pen to bring forth its ink.

"D-U-N-G." The letters are said slowly to keep time with Jennifer's hand. Only after it is written does Jennifer seem to look at the name. This scene has played out many a day in her lifetime. It was worst in middle school when the already low brow humor met up with the pre-teen ability to search a dictionary. Even in adulthood she'd watch people pronounce her name correctly while reading it, trying to break their mind's habit of using western phonetics so as not to embarrass her, but mostly not to embarrass themselves. For a time, she'd spelt out "Yoom" in her correspondence. She'd place it in the middle of her name the same way she'd put a bit of brisket in pho. Anglos always focus on the meat, little more than garnish, not appreciating how the broth makes the dish. Dung's practiced polite smile emerges to make her hostess feel comfortable, but Dung decides she will correct Jennifer.

"Dung," Jennifer says with perfect pronunciation, without the need of correction, "you're going to sit by me since you are my honored guest." Jennifer looks her up and down, before meeting Dung's eyes for the first time. "Well, you're not dressed at all." Dung looks down at her light hemp button up and her breathable recycled nylon pants. Jennifer heads for the stairs but Dung interrupts with the same raised palm she used for her children. The command stops Jennifer. Dung produces her family's jade bracelet from the velvet bag in her pocket and puts it on her wrist.

"Well, that's nice but it's not enough."

A knock at the door replaces a response about how the bracelet's weight of importance makes it more than enough. Jennifer opens the door to find a man whose thinning grey hair, thicker grey beard, hooked nose, red face, and barrel chest all look familiar. Even his wicking polo and vinyl loafers look familiar. His name is John, and he's familiar because he lives one street over and walks every evening at this hour. In his hand is a very familiar looking suitcase. It's Dung's. She opens it to find all her most prized possessions, including her red áo dài. Her children must have watched her walk to this house and left it here for her. Jennifer spies it from over her shoulder.

"There you go, honey. Go put that on. What'd you say your name is…John? You staying for dinner?"

"Can't say I've got other dinner plans."

Dung complies and goes upstairs to put her *áo dài* on, just so she can feel something familiar at this strange time, in this strange house, with these strange people. She can't help but wonder what her children thought as she walked away from them. Was this suitcase a last attempt to make their mother happy? Such a kind gesture. Or could it even be their blessing for her decision? Leaving this means they won't carry anything of hers. Her son will always sneeze like her. Her daughter will always rub her left earlobe when she's worried, just like Dung's mother did. Seems a shame they won't keep pictures on their person as she has. But maybe it's better this way. Without something to carry, nothing will weigh you down. Then maybe they won't feel like they're running, only leaving. By the time Dung returns, Jennifer has scrawled John's name on the card, and he's seated at the table. Despite not knowing his name seven minutes earlier, they are laughing hysterically.

"Dung, my love! You look perfect! Now come sit down and eat. It's getting cold. John here lives on our street. He decided to stay for the hurricane, too. Said he smelled all that food and figured someone was having a hurricane party and he didn't want to miss out. Now, what's your partner gonna think if you don't get them over here."

"She'd be happy. She's gone, dead about three years now," John says.

"I'm sorry about that," Jennifer says, not sorry at all.

"What about the rest of your family?" Dung asks with genuine concern.

"Don't got any. Part of why I decided to stay."

Dung looks down, feeling sorry for a person without family. A pang of guilt erupts in her gut. The connection to her family and past she'd felt while slipping into her *áo dài* dissipates. She sent her family away. At the time it seemed right to stop all this running and give them an unfettered life. Now she wonders if she saddled them with more hurt and regret. She thinks she should message them.

"John, you got any drugs?" Jennifer asks. The brashness interrupts Dung's feelings.

"As a matter of fact, I do. Bought a whole bunch of MDMA and was going to do it all tonight and through the storm. I'd be happy to share."

"Well, shit! Go get it! And do it fast so this food doesn't get any colder!"

After John leaves, Dung again thinks about her family. She didn't stop to ask what they would want or need. Her poor son is so sensitive. This is probably hard on him.

"I'm gonna fuck him," Jennifer announces before gulping down an entire glass of wine. Dung again is dumbfounded by her brazenness. The older woman doesn't seem to care at all what others think of her. And why should she? This is most likely her last night on earth. Jennifer leans into the finality, embracing the way it unshackles the weight of life from her. That sort of freedom is beautiful to Dung. Jennifer watches her for some sort of response. Dung musters her most polite smile.

"Enjoy," she tells her elder.

"You need to enjoy, too, honey. Get some more weed. Drink some more. This is how you do a hurricane!" Dung could not imagine denying her gracious elder. As they pass the dab pen back and forth, John walks back in, wearing slightly better clothes than before. Behind him is a small, balding, yet young man. His ochre eyes open wide over his long round nose, as if constantly surprised. Between the big eyes, and his tawny, multi-racial skin, he seems like a scared little finch to Dung. The bird holds up a keg with a dolly.

"Jennifer. Mrs. Nguyen. This is Marcus. He is my neighbor a couple of doors down. You mind if he joins us?"

Jennifer's eyes sparkle. "Not at all, sugar. Pull up a chair and let me write you a name card."

They settle in and pick apart the pile of meat. Never has Dung eaten only meat at a meal. It has never been central to her cooking. With the national attitude seeing meat as gluttonous and inhumane, she'd removed it almost completely from her diet (except for her traditional dishes like *thít kho* or *bánh tét* at *Tet*, of course). The thick beer only serves to fill her more. Her stomach reacts in shock. By the end of the meal, she is glad life is ending so she doesn't feel this miserable for much longer. She is glad the conversation was light during the meal. Her unassuming and pleasant expression, paired with her introverted nature, usually encourages the average person to talk beyond reasonable limits. Instead, they all rub their tummies quietly. It's space enough for Dung to fully appreciate the guests at the table, the last people she'll see in this life. They're likely thinking the same, judging by their heavy silence. Several minutes pass before Jennifer brings the conversation back.

"What's your story, Marcus?"

"What do you mean?"

"I mean, why are you still here with the rest of life's rejects?"

"Oh. Well…see, I was going to kill myself. Lost my job a month ago and my husband decided to leave me after that. But I'm such a wimp. Then this storm popped up in the gulf and the problem was solved for me. I've been working on that keg since yesterday. So…you know."

Everyone returns to silence for a moment. Marcus looks down, as if wanting to die before the storm is something to be ashamed of now. Dung starts to tell him how she is choosing the storm because it is the first time she has ever gotten to live, but she is cut off.

"Well I'm glad you came here to hang out with us, honey. You're not going out with a frown I can tell you that much," Jennifer says. John cocks back his beer in agreement and hoots. Everyone else follows suit. They adjourn back outside where night has settled in. Thick clouds appear and the wind is near constant. The weather report is still projected onto the wall. The rainbow-colored 3D Model titled "Hurricane Yara" in big white letters gives the backyard the ambiance of a night club. All four watch, drinking keg beer, entranced.

When she was a child, her grandmother said the breezes are different here. At first, Dung thought she meant they were not as hot or humid. But tonight, she understands the wind feels different because her family was always moving with the wind, changing with them. Now, sitting here with misfits and watching the rainbow wheel of the storm spin slowly toward them, she knows the wind moves over and around her because she is stationary. Knowing no one has felt the wind this way in three generations loosens something in her. A moan reaches her ears. She thinks it is the sound of her glacial past shifting. After the third moan, John confirms he hears them also and determines that they are happening opposite the rhythm of the breathing wind. He also pinpoints their origin from next door. They watch as John struggles over the fence. Several long minutes pass before he returns with a disheveled young woman, roughly the age Dung's grandmother would have been when she arrived here. The young woman is crying. Despite the humidity, Dung instinctually wraps the girl in the blanket she found nearby in a waterproof chest.

"He has to come back. It's going to be bad," the young white girl sobs.

"Who?" Dung asks.

"Lenny. My dog. He ran away yesterday, right as I was packing up. I've looked all over. I can't leave without him." The way "leave" drops with a southern drawl makes it sound like "live."

Dung wraps her arms around the young girl and begins to rock. The girl's mess of dirty blond hair falls against Dung's *áo dài*. Dark circles under the young woman's eyes deepen as the sob descends into her chest and tears fall down her small nose. Dung imagines this is what Jennifer might have looked like in her younger years. They even share hazel eyes. The sound of the forlorn, hopeless sobs for Lenny penetrates Dung's body. From deep in her soul, her own tears well up. Dung's body has been the caretaker of her ancestors' tears; tears made of lives not fully lived, starvation, Communists, and leaving everything and everyone for unknown lands. With the running having stopped, something in Dung's chest breaks free and she loses herself in her own flood, tears with enough water to refill the distance crossed between Vietnam and America, and then enough more to make a hurricane. This working and running, only to have Earth's weather war continue taking her homes, and her life, stops here. She will no longer feel guilt for setting her children free. When her tears finally slow, she perceives arms and hands around her, wiping her tears and squeezing her tightly. Her eyes focus on the origin of the tightest arms, ones belonging to the young white girl wrapped in this sweaty, humid blanket cocoon with her. All comfort Dung, intermittently wiping their own tears. Dung has arrived, without her children, and with her ancestors. She knows this is the only way it could happen.

"What's your name, sugar?" Jennifer asks the newest member of this strange tribe.

"Ensley."

"Ensley," Jennifer begins as if she's said the name every day of her life, "let's get really fucked up."

The MDMA is the highest potency, John says. He's quickly proven right. All of them lay in the grass, feeling everything. The drinking and the marijuana were manufactured feelings, but this feels unlike anything Dung has experienced. The biggest side effect of always running is you can never stop for love. There's no time to love when you are surviving. There is only enough time to give everything in hopes something survives. After her flood of tears, the MDMA brings her ashore into a love she's never known. She thinks of her grandmother, her mother, and instead of wondering if she has done them proud, she can only love them. She thinks of her children, going to find their homes, and instead of fear and guilt, she feels love. Then there is a person she has not thought much of despite spending her whole life with her: Dung. She thinks of her life, the running, the surviving, the overcoming, and feels deep, tremendous love. It's over now. She's made it. She has reached the end of the world. A smile, rooted in her soul, breaks on her face. She pulls the picture of her young grandmother from her pocket to look a last time. Dung has finally mimicked her smile. This is how far she had to come to undo the past. A picture flashes in her mind of Amon and Amelia, driving to safety, returning to a home. With perfect confidence, absolute solace, she knows the running has stopped. She knows because she has found her home.

At the edge of the yard, a pale figure moves against the wind. Dung's eyes are drawn to it and finally focus to see Ensley standing naked, wind blowing through her dirty blonde hair. Her upper left buttock sports a birthmark, similar in shape to Dung's intertwined tattoo of Vietnam and Orleans Parish. She is not shocked. She is home, after all, and this coincidence is just confirmation the past has finally resolved; a sign all those ancestors returned home as she has. Neither is she shocked to look to her left and see Jennifer also naked, save for the tiara jostling on her head. Her nearly ninety-year-old tattooed body bounces on top of John's reddening naked body, red as the storm. Dung's Southern judgement for Jennifer's lack of restraint must have washed away with the tears, leaving only acceptance in its wake. She marvels that love now fills the spaces in her, where regrets, longings, and perceived shortcomings once lived. Where she does find shock is to her right with a pair of smitten bird eyes peering at her. They no longer look afraid. She'd seen eyes like these once before, on a now deceased husband on the day of their wedding.

"Would you?" Marcus asks, very sweetly, very genuinely. It takes a moment to understand through her fog of love, through the breaking of the world, what he is asking. A last gift from my ancestors, she thinks; someone to find me beautiful. But Dung cannot accept an invitation to sex. Here, at the end of things, she's been given everything she's desired. It would be impolite to take everything, letting her ancestors, or maybe even God, believe they had not given her enough. She smiles a warm motherly smile, something she'd wanted to do so many more times in her life. She glances over his shoulder to the naked beauty behind him. The bird follows her gaze, before looking back to Dung, fear haunting his eyes once more. Dung smiles again, reassuringly. He rises and walks over to Ensley. Dung turns her back on them to watch the weather map still projected on the house. The wind is now a constant roar, masking the sounds of love being made on both sides of her.

The wheel spins as more up to date images amend its path. She considers turning up the volume but decides not to interrupt the love. As the rainbow changes to only red, the spinning mass hypnotizes her. She lovingly strokes the jade bracelet on her wrist. Her eyes venture from the red map to her own red *áo dài*. It looks brighter, cleaner, like a sad memory has been washed away by the impending waves already. The happiness of home is her final accessory. She thinks even Jennifer would find it to be enough. She does not notice when the lovemaking stops, some party members now dressed, and all sitting around her in the grass. Jennifer takes the initiative to raise the volume just in time to hear the updated trajectory.

Strike a Chord

Twelve flash drives, seventy-two CDs, thirty-one vinyl albums, an accordion, and four unopened packs of men's underwear arrive at Gladys's door. From the look of the models on the packaging, not to mention the cardboard inserts, the underwear has been stored since some time in the 2020s. She looks through the obscure music collection, and then back at the underwear, trying to figure out which friend is pranking her and what the prank is even supposed to mean. The mystery remains even after Moniqua returns home from the doctor. She's relieved Gladys wants to figure this out rather than hound her with questions about her treatment.

It is a phone call from Gladys's mom which clears up the confusion. Gladys's seventy-year-old second cousin died last month, and his will was specific about leaving Glady's all his music and clothes. Parker had come through Austin several years ago, wanting to visit the Live Music Capital of the World before he got too old to take in the fabled music scene. He'd been just as disappointed as Gladys and her wife to find the city still struggling with its identity. Was it the Live Music Capital, the Beer Capital, or the Tech Capital? He said his favorite parts of the trip were the times they'd talked about music and fashion. After pancreatic cancer wasted him away in a matter of months, he decided to memorialize the only time he'd met Gladys by giving her his music and clothes. Except the latter had not been properly stored in the Louisiana humidity, and all his garments mildewed, except for these packs of old unopened underwear.

Gladys has no problem throwing the underwear away but wonders how long she'll have to hang on to the rest of this crap in her modest home to stave off her mother's offense. That timeline may not coincide with her wife's irritation of how much space it takes up; irritation already apparent on her face. They are trying to have a baby, after all, complete with all the baby stuff, and their condo apartment is already cramped. The old uninsulated garage/music studio is the best place for it. Hopefully, the lack of insulation will mean the material will succumb to the humidity in Austin which nearly matches Louisiana's.

Parker had specific musical tastes judging by what's on the flash drives. The CDs and vinyl contain only Louisiana Cajun and Creole music. Between an excuse to use her antique record player, and an attempt to give Moniqua her space following the doctor's appointment, she decides to see what the black vinyl has to offer. After some warm pops from the needle, she hears the beginning of "Colinda." Her ears are instantly disoriented by the French language wrapped around the honking of an accordion. The awkward sounds roll out in 4/4 time, accented by the croak and thrum of alternating bass keys. It's happy, but also a little mischievous. She smiles, looking into the cavernous air duct of her portable AC, air blowing her thin blonde hair. She turns the music to max to hear it over the air. An English version of the verse follows the French, confirming the lyrics are in fact naughty; a provocative dance stolen with Colinda to make "the old ladies mad" while Colinda's mother is away. Its simplicity is infectious. It's so unlike anything in her complex life right now.

The accordion glints from inside the box she'd placed on the shelf. It has a mother-of-pearl cover and keys yellowed from use. It's a shame to keep something this loved and cared for in a box hidden away. She pulls it down and unhooks the bellows strap. It opens with a drawn-out organ sound, groaning and grating nerves still frayed from having to store unwanted objects. She fingers the keys and realizes quickly there is little difference from playing a piano. Another few plays of the record and she nearly has the bass buttons figured out. It's a very intuitive instrument. The sun is down, and she is drenched in sweat, before she senses her wife in the garage doorway.

"It sounds like you're killing cats in here," Moniqua says without any attempt at humor. Her pale green nightgown drapes over her short frame, matching her synthetic silk head wrap.

"Sorry. Got carried away," Gladys replies in her airy, yet direct way.

"Uh-huh. If you're going to keep playing, can you plug in some headphones or something?" The way Moniqua says "playing" sounds less about music and more about Gladys's direction in life.

The musician pushes the sweaty blonde hair off her forehead, thankful that she cut it even shorter than usual. "This doesn't have a headphone jack. Can you put in your earplugs like you used to when we first got married? I think I'm figuring something out in here."

Moniqua looks at her incredulously for a long time while Gladys stares back with unwavering seafoam green eyes. "I need sleep," Moniqua states flatly before turning and leaving.

There is no "good night" or "I love you." Gladys can't win. When she tries to be an attentive wife, give Moniqua massages, cook her favorite meals, ask about the shots to her stomach or the bruises, she is smothering. Now, as she instead focuses on her own work and happiness, she is both too much and too little. This started with the home study to see if they are fit to have a child. Despite it being a government prerequisite to getting a parent license, Moniqua took it personal, creating a whirlpool of insecurity about the type of mother she'd be. Could she live up to her own mother's legacy? Within moments of meeting her mother-in-law, Gladys could tell that Moniqua's mother never made a parenting mistake. Then Moniqua's first failed IVF procedure happened, and Gladys could not do anything right. Ten years of blissful marriage was upended by doctor visits filled with detailed conversations about her wife's highly selective uterus and percentages on whether their duo would become a trio. But there was never a discussion about who would carry the baby. Moniqua needs to feel the baby grow inside her, to know her child implicitly. Gladys didn't object because Moniqua's reasoning is part of what makes her a perfect parent already. It's these things that make Moniqua opposite from any adult in Gladys's broken past.

A silent worry gnaws at Gladys. She's frightened she'll turn out to be a parent like hers were, always too much or too little, never just right. She worries her child will end up feeling as lonely as she was before Moniqua. The emptiness her wife left in the doorway when she went to bed makes her feel lonely now. Music has always kept her company. Tonight, it will be her haven in unwantedness. She hopes the need for this haven is temporary.

The chords of "Colinda" are simple, though she must play them again and again to get them right on the new instrument. She tries to replicate the French words; glad she picked a one verse song to start with. The conversation (or was it a scolding) with her wife replays in her head, specifically the words "first got married." She even sings it as part of the song inadvertently.

Their start was forbidden. She'd been Moniqua's boss at the vegan restaurant they worked in during their twenties. Both shared a love of meat products, which then turned into a real, deep love Gladys didn't think possible from all her previous relationships built out of settling. In only two dates, Gladys understood Moniqua's rarity. Gladys was the first woman Moniqua had been with. They read books, watched documentaries, and visited iconic places of the Queer Rights Movement. Gladys proposed in front of Stonewall. Their early years were filled as much with fists in the air as love in their hearts. As she continues to sing "Colinda," the angst connected to the punk music she is used to playing is replaced by a sweet angelic sound she didn't know she possessed. French words begin to feel natural, almost like she's speaking a tongue merely forgotten. Colinda's name is uttered intimately and tenderly. Eventually she feels she is singing to Colinda, instead of about her.

Between the memories of their rebel love, and swirling images of what she believes a young, vibrant, and daring Colinda might have looked like, Gladys gets an idea. A smile curls the ends of her small, unassuming mouth as she looks up the French translation for "man" and "father." Her hands finally able to make the chords in succession, she flicks on the camera of her roll up interface. In moments she records "Colinda" with the same playfulness and mischievousness the song was meant to embody, but converts it into an anthem against the patriarchy. She sings about stealing a dance with her young female lover to make "all the old men mad." Perceivable in her tone, and by her slightly diminished tempo, is a voice singing to someone they know intrinsically. Gladys's delicate smile turns her thin Swedish cheeks further upward as she replays the video of herself, hemp tee shirt and blonde hair plastered against her in sweat. Her wet, dimly lit image inside a garage not retrofitted for climate, laboriously playing an awkward instrument, and using a language she'd learned only a few hours ago, feels more punk than anything she's created with guitars or a music program. Clicking off the camera, she uploads the recording to the "Regional Singer/Songwriter" YouTube channel she's not used since IVF started. Her good mood is washed away in the shower by the dry hygiene powder. She audibly curses the dry bed of the Lake Travis Reservoir and its inability to provide a final cleanse. She crawls in bed at 5:02 AM.

Moniqua is gone when Gladys wakes up. The earplugs on the nightstand could mean Moniqua used them and just set them down afterwards, or thought they were useless and she ended up taking them out. Guilt rises at the thought of her scared and tired partner staying up all night listening to her wife struggle with an accordion. Playing until the sun comes up is a life she'd be happy to return to. But this loneliness, feeling abandoned, set against heartless disregard of the needs of others, is not her. The song started this weird detour. Gladys decides to delete the recording and then destroy the records next. When she opens her roll up interface to her entry, she stops at the delete confirmation when the view count catches her eye: 32,407 since 5AM. She falls into her chair, her seafoam eyes locked on the number. In the years she's been posting to this and seventeen other channels she has never had so many view counts in a year, much less six hours. Persistent chiming from her watch interface catches her attention. They start to roll in at a pace she can't keep up with. Dozens of texts and video chats later and she's asked by the Southern Arm of the LGBTQIA+ Rights Association to use it as the anthem for gay pride month to recognize the historical and multicultural roots of the organization in this region. Emails request interviews about how she'd found this song, and to talk about the inspiration for the small, yet important changes. She answers texts from songwriting friends, talking about how poignant this song is, how beautiful. The accordion added an intimacy to the recording, something almost maternal, as she cradled and rocked the instrument in her arms. Her modifications remind them of the common fight they continue since oppressors just get cleverer in their abilities to obfuscate and bury their meanings. It doesn't matter if a trans-identified person held the office of President of the United States before the current idiot, the attempts to silence voices like Gladys's are out there. By the time Moniqua comes home from her contract tech support job with groceries in her arms Gladys is giddy.

"Babe! I recorded this random song last night after I learned the accordion and it's gone national! I got people from all over texting and emailing and sharing. Big organizations want to use it!"

A patient, yet fake, smile rests on Moniqua's face as she waits for Gladys to finish. "I'm glad your song is popular. And I saw it went national. Have you seen *everything* people are saying?"

"What do you mean?"

"You haven't looked at the comments, have you?" Moniqua puts the groceries down as Gladys goes back to her interface. "The doctor's office didn't call or message, did they?"

Gladys cannot hear her. She's already speed reading through comments. Most are in support and after twenty-five in a row of this nature she wonders if Moniqua just doesn't want to praise what kept her up all night. Then she sees it:

"@NoMysteryinHistory708: Cute reframe of the song, but this is completely out of context. @Gladitsus doesn't even acknowledge the time in which Colinda was made or what the song meant for the ethnic group it was written for. This is just another person re-writing the past through irresponsible use of the 'artistic license.' Visit my page 'From was to is' to read more on this tendency in recent music and art."

And then:

"@xxFreefromtheSouthxx: Appropriation at its best. @Gladitsus you just stole something that had been stolen before. Just like an oppressor to cover their tracks with more oppression."

"Did the doctor call, hon?"

"What are they talking about?" Gladys asks rhetorically as she searches the origin of the song. She learns it was an

African war dance combined with stick fighting. The Cajuns and Creoles must have found the Afro Caribbean version of this dance "provocative" and wrote this little ditty. "This wasn't appropriation of appropriation, was it?"

"Babe! The Doctor!"

"Huh? No. No call."

Moniqua walks from the kitchen with her hand on her hip. "You're something else. Two days ago I couldn't get you out of my ass. Now you can't be bothered to find out if the gene therapy they did is going to work."

"Wait, what? I thought you said you'd never do gene therapy."

"I had to make a change. This whole process is killing me." Gladys raises her slender but broad frame from the couch with a look of compassion. Moniqua is having none of this either. "And yes, it's appropriating twice over. But I'm not worried about that right now. I'm worried about the negative attention this thing is getting. We don't need that right now."

Glady's shoulders slump as she feels, again, she cannot win. "So, you do know what we need. Could you share?"

Moniqua's hand drops from her hip in exasperation. "I'm going get my nails done," she says before walking out the door.

House to herself, and impossibility eroding the dry ground beneath her, Gladys reads every single comment. She reads the new ones as they come in. Still most are in support, remarking on how'd they'd never known of this music, how the phrasing is melancholic and soothing, the French words harkening back to something lost in us. The melodies uncover what's hidden. Some say she is modernizing these songs to make them current and real. But there is a growing contingency of dissonance. Of course, she feels what all artists do, that the dissonance is just people who don't get her work. Swallowing her ego, she accepts that she needs to be more mindful of the work she chooses to emulate or alter.

But there is something else there, something sinister. She re-reads the trolls over and over until she realizes it: it's all veiled oppression, homophobia, and sexism. While people hide behind history, gaslighting by calling her the oppressor, they are only attempting to put her back in her place, or at least what they think is her place. A late night's decision in a garage unleashed what she's spent her identity fighting against. Realizing this means the only course of action is to continue.

On a hill overlooking the desiccated pines of Bastrop right at sunset, Gladys centers the camera of her roll-up interface on her. The Saharan dust lends hues of pink and gold to the sun behind her, which keeps her in shadow. This is by design. She wants this to be about the music. Following an afternoon of perusing records, she found another song in both English and French. More importantly, she found something which embodies her rebellion, something she doesn't need to alter, so she'd only sing through appreciation instead of appropriation: Bonsoir, Catin's *Faut tu Voir*. She sings louder to overcome the muffle of the mask helping her breathe through the wildfire smoke and ozone inundating Austin this time of year. Her goggles make it hard to see the notes on the screen. Her silhouette squeezes the bellows dramatically, making the accordion rasp and growl. Defiance and vulnerability extract the punk in her lungs as she shrieks, "Il faut me sauver de cette ball and chain/It's a free world baby/Je me sens comme un prisonnier." After five takes, mainly because of the wind ruining the sound, the sun sets behind her. She strips her stifling UV protective shirt and wipes the sticky sunscreen from her face before posting the best of the takes.

At home, Moniqua has already gone to bed. Gladys stands at the doorway watching her eyebrows furrow in her sleep, hoping the furrow isn't for her. Moniqua's brown skin glows in the hallway light. The little curl that always makes its way out of her silk headwrap dances in fan breezes. Gladys lovingly looks at her lips, remembers how they felt the first time, and every time ever since. Music was supposed to be shared with her wife, especially since this is one of the biggest things they connected over. Moniqua should sing with her. Instead, this beautiful music, its mischievousness and irreverence, the way it connects back to a place in her life where things made sense, is just an inconvenience. Moniqua's life is diverging. Gladys retreats to her garage and puts on Feufollet's 2015 album. As she listens through the years of this music, she ponders on how it evolves yet manages to hold onto the essence that gives it its identity. If this were something she could learn to do, her marriage would feel cohesive like the culture this music sings about.

Lost in French and accordions, she forgets she posted something at sundown. She wipes the sweat from her forehead, pushes the little portable AC unit to its lowest setting, and unfurls her roll-up interface. Her second posting has garnered her subscribers. It's an anomaly on this channel since most people subscribe to sterilized pop/country/hip hop now. She goes back to "Colinda" from the day before, now added to a sub-Reddit, and sees her rebellion has grown and comrades have come to her defense against trolls. Her version of the song is a "cry out against the darkness of history," and "a homing beacon for those seeking a new era," "melding the feminine spirit with soul of resistance," "wrapped in a melody both timeless and mesmerizing." r/CovxnofWomxn sums up much of what Gladys believes when she writes "This music simultaneously reminds us of where we've been and why we can't go back. Patriarchy is the root of the global climate crisis. Womxn seek to give and not to take. We should never hide our love, grace, and power. The world needs us to lead it through this era. This song is a beautiful example of how a little more discomfort in the past could have given us more life to work with today." As she reads charged, yet hilarious, counterattacks (especially the one likening the previous centuries of all straight male leadership to watching the last season of the Simpsons in '64 on mute), a notification appears for a new comment on the most recent post.

"r/Francophilebythemile: I really like this version, and judging by what I've read about Bonsoir, Catin, they would've liked it, too. But you're not creating from within the culture. You're just using it as a vehicle, and that's disrespectful. This song is made to preserve roots by growing new branches. Your little cutting, your weekend interpretation, can't be in the same camp as this song. You are curating nothing. You advance confusion about this music."

With eyes welling up, Gladys knows the comments are right. These are more tears than a troll should be able to pull, though. After several moments spent with her hands over the interface keyboard, staving off the urge to respond, the meaning finds her. Her life is about trying to participate, to finally be part of something meaningful, and become someone. This marriage is meaningful, making her a wife. This child will be meaningful, making her a mother. She's searched for roles to turn her into someone, destroying her fractured history and accompanying loneliness. The verge of participating in something meaningful always makes excitement take over and she can't help herself, overshooting what others get implicitly. With Moniqua she tries to get info out of her about how IVF is going, like she thinks a wife should. But too many questions take her out of the realm of partner and mom and make her into an interrogator. Retreat always seems like the best option when that happens, but then she ends up overcorrecting, wallowing in self-pity and frustration. Staring through salty eyes she contemplates retreating from this music. She could ghost the internet. But that wouldn't solve anything. Not participating just ensures she will never be real, meaningful, or understood. Besides, in this case it would let ignorance stew and that's not an option.

Unlike Moniqua, who doesn't have a search tab, she can do things to better understand this music and connect with it. She scrolls through several other sub-Reddits and YouTube Regional Channels until she finally finds what she is looking for. This one podcast comes out of Louisiana and focuses on the history of the region, as told by a Cajun man. She binges nearly the entire first season for the cadence of his words, the humor, and his wisdom. Even though she doesn't always get his references, he seems to hold the meaning of this music. His easy-going attitude, his humor, all speak of a person who gets life just right. He understands who he is and what that means. Before she has a chance to talk herself out of it, she direct messages the producer and rolls up the interface. By the time she gets into her bed, Moniqua has already left for work.

The unforgiving Austin sun slices through the self-regulating tint of Gladys's ultra-efficient windows. It takes her a few moments to remember why she is waking up in the afternoon again. After her shot of syn espresso, she opens her interface to find the producer of the Cajun/Creole in the twenty-first show has responded. He writes Mr. Michot would be happy to sing a duet with her for an upcoming podcast since music is not a territory they'd covered much of yet. It's crazy, even stupid, to try and capitalize on five minutes of fame with a stranger, singing music which isn't hers, while her wife toils in baby limbo. But if she could get this music right, Gladys thinks, take something old and make it new, fighting the patriarchy in the process, maybe she could do the same for her stormy marriage and figure how to be a real mom. The latter can't be too different than nurturing a budding movement. Gladys texts Moniqua from the road in her Google sedan, telling her she'll be home late again. Around Buffalo, TX she receives a screen call from Moniqua.

"So you're just going to leave and tell me after you've already left?"

"I'm not leaving, Moniqua. Just want to take this chance, be part of something bigger than me."

"That's what I want, too. But you keep acting weird."

"Me? *Me*? I can't do right by you lately."

"Because you're not acting like you."

"This music is bringing me back to the old me. So we can be the old us."

"You have lost your mind," Moniqua says running her hand over her face in exasperation. The lab diamonds from her wedding ring twinkle in the artificial light of her screen depicting Gladys's image.

"Tell me we'll come back," Gladys begs.

"Tell me you'll come back," Moniqua requests after too long a pause.

"I'll be back tomorrow."

"We'll talk about us then." The screen is black before Gladys can even think to respond.

The self-drive still estimates over an hour. She unbuckles her accordion, holding it as she would an infant. The smooth mother-of-pearl winks from underneath her hands as she continues to practice. It's easier to work the bellows and manage the keys. In the short time she's taken to learn this instrument, she's come to understand how much she's underestimated it. It can breathe, nearly on its own. It has a depth able to create multiple tones, modified by the slightest movement. It can be simple, or very complex, with very little effort.

Absorbed in her appreciation of its versatility, she doesn't notice the change in the landscape. She's crossed the lengthened bridge over the ever-widening Toledo Bend Reservoir. The groves of live oaks are exchanged for forests which more closely resemble jungle. The air quality, too, has changed. Her thin hair begins to frizz in unimaginable humidity, something she didn't think was possible. Most troubling of changes, though, is the lack of civilization. Few buildings are seen from the highway. Even in Buffalo there were several communities. It appears to Gladys that her cousin, the one who started this journey with underwear and music, may have died of loneliness as much as anything else. Time and place are on the move backward here.

When she arrives at the modest studio, she is greeted by Jamil, the podcast producer of Cajun/Creole in the twenty-first. She apologizes for her lack of experience with her instrument and lets him know she's only learned two songs, which are proportional to the number of days she has been playing. Jamil tells her he's come to appreciate anything which respects and cherishes this culture, even if it is not authentic. Without fanfare, he introduces her to Ben Michot, the keeper of Cajun lore and culture, as well as the last known speaker of Louisiana French.

"Jamil tells me we'll be singing a song." Gladys's mouth drops open. He has none of the Cajun accent she'd seen on the show. He's an imposter. How easily she, an imposter in her own right, has been sucked in by another. "I overheard what you told Jamil. I only know a few songs, myself. It's been a long time since I've sung any of them. How about we sing 'Jolie Blonde?' Seems fitting given my current company."

Jamil's hands fly across the keyboard as he produces the sheet music and projects it on the wall. Ben starts to tap the beat with his foot, waiting for her to follow with the accordion chords. She didn't expect them to jump right in like this. An attempt at a smile comes out as a wince. Gladys tries to play but her hands struggle across the instrument. She misses notes. Her timing is off. Here it is again. She's been too much, missed what this music is. The notes won't come out because they don't belong to her. So desperate to become part of something, she's become a cheap, empty replica. She's no more able to pick up a new instrument, embody age-old music to create a movement, than she is able to create a life and raise it built on a relationship where she can barely take care of one person's expectations and happiness. She couldn't appreciate what being a wife and a mother means for the same reason she couldn't understand what her commenters were saying about this music: it's deeper and you must play from the places in your soul you've never explored. Gladys realizes that she busied herself with the feelings and thoughts of others, safely hiding behind acceptance and social movement. When she goes to look inside for what she can authentically bring to life, she isn't sure of what's there. Before she can help it, her chest caves in. Hands coming down, her face turns the pallor of her mother-of-pearl accordion. She hides her eyes from being seen by them.

"Are you ok?" Ben asks with genuine concern.

"I'm sorry. This…I'm…it's not going to work. This isn't my music. I've made a mistake, and I've wasted your time."

Ben smiles and looks over at Jamil, who in turn wears a somber face. "We heard your other two songs. You feel Cajun to me." Another look to Jamil and the speakers let loose a pure accordion track in 3/4 time.

"Hey, jolie 'tite blonde!" rings from Ben Michot in a perfect Cajun accent. His voice borders on a wail, pining away for the one who left him. She still doesn't know enough French to translate his words, but she doesn't have to. The lonesomeness in his voice gives sound to what she's felt since she was a child. Tears rim her eyes as the well of emptiness empties, somehow becoming full in the process. This man, who apparently is not Cajun, can step inside this world and become it, and it becomes him. He sings effortlessly, the words, the accent, the music coming from within without trying, until Gladys can no longer hide her eyes. With every line, each word he cries out, he becomes more complete. She remains silent as the song finishes. The man she now sees he is not an imposter, but someone who has found meaning all his own in someone else's melodies.

"You see," he says, again without a trace of Cajun accent, "you have to feel it. Put all of you into it. Don't hesitate. Know who you are singing the song to."

She played this music to conjure a past and create a movement. But really, it's for someone. "Colinda" was rewritten as she thought of Moniqua and how to reconnect with her when words and actions failed. Her green eyes glisten and her small mouth widens in a grin. She remembers why she was attracted to this music in the first place. It touched her anger, her wonder, her mischievousness, and now her loneliness, and made her know all of it is real. It's something she didn't have to think about, which is why she was able to learn it so fast, why it spurned her to play and create. The music found what is genuine in her and brought it forward. It brokered a deal between the uncertain future and the cemented past, making it finally feel like where she is, what she is, is just right.

HER CAR PARKS ITSELF IN FRONT of their apartment as she re-listens to the episode where she played with Ben. Jamil is an excellent editor, weaving her story into Michot's. There are so many similarities it makes her wish she'd watched all the episodes of the show before she emailed Jamil. She wouldn't have wasted time feeling insecure and confused. She would have asked Ben some real questions. "No," she says aloud to herself. "It was just right." Retraining her focus on the task at hand, she unlocks the front door and places her accordion on the stairs. Moniqua is cozied up on the couch in the living room, already in her pajamas, hair wrap on. She turns off her interface as Gladys walks up. Gladys drops a greasy bag of lukewarm turkey neck jambalaya from Hendrick's on the coffee table before her.

"I need—" Moniqua begins.

"Let me. I'm sorry about the last few days. You're already an amazing wife. You'll be an amazing mom. I don't know how to do both of those things yet. But I'm going to stop trying to be something, trying to participate in this family, stop running away when I get scared, and just be. I will find a way to weave the old me and the new me together so we can be a good us."

Moniqua smiles while tears begin to fall down her face. "We're pregnant," she says. Gladys doesn't move from the opening to the living room. Moniqua continues to cry and smile until the inertia Gladys had been cast in gives way. Gladys embraces and kisses her wife, breathing in the scent of her shea butter and the smell of the beautiful, perfect mother beneath it, before collapsing on the couch together. Glady's head now rests on Moniqua's chest and she can hear her heart beating in 4/4 time. "We are a good 'us'," Moniqua begins, her heartbeat setting the pace for Gladys's own heart. "I didn't need the edited version of you. I need the 'you' I married. The 'you' I need to be a mom with. When you started trying too hard, when you left, you stopped being you. I'm so glad you're back." She exhales. While she can't see Gladys's face, Moniqua can feel her wife's body on top of her shudder as Gladys cries. "I want you to name her," Moniqua tells her.

"You already know she's a she?" Gladys asks, sitting up and wiping her tears.

"Yeah."

Gladys goes back to the stairs for her accordion and sits again in front of Moniqua. She smiles at her wife's quizzical face before resting her eyes on Moniqua's tummy and the little life beginning inside. Their baby has amazing sense of cadence, stoking a rebellion against her moms' timing, knowing just when to release tension. But she'll provoke. Never will she bend to excuses like "we've always done it that way." She will be a warrior, even a general, who'll take the old and dance it into the new, making something perfect.

Gladys knows just what name to give her. Opening the bellows, she sings sweetly:

> *Allons danser, Colinda*
> *Danser collé, Colinda*
> *Pendant ta mère n'est pas là*
> *Pour faire facher les vielles femmes*
> *C'est pas tout le monde qui peut danser*
> *Toutes les vielles valses du vieux temps*
> *Pendant 'ta mère n'est pas là*
> *Allons danser, Colinda!*

River Card

"Once the sea trickled into New York, once Houston was saturated, and San Francisco took their tech inland to the Dakotas and Utah and Nevada—the Gulf Coast, and Louisiana specifically—we became the nation's wet basement. Why were we so easy to throw away? When New Orleans was dry, the nation loved us. When oil was king, the U.S. couldn't get enough of us. Now Texas won't even give us love. Our population is aging or leaving. One more Category 6 hurricane like Pilar and this won't even be a place anymore. It will be a port. A rest stop. What did we do to deserve this? Did we show you too good of a time? If that's the case, just remember, even sex workers get paid."

"Now Mr. Governor, you can't say we don't have national prominence anymore. A quick survey of the big five social medias still have Louisiana trending in extinction tourism, music, food, even cultural channels."

"Our culture, like the rest of this state, is getting watered down. Our food gets blander by the year since people think flavor is greedy. Some Texas woman was playing our Cajun music like it was her own. Extinction tourism is a boutique industry at best. And if you are referencing the man who doesn't know what he's saying in our French patois…just don't. If anything, you're proving my point. This state, this history, and the soul it brings to the nation and the world, is drowning. And no one seems to care."

"You've been listening to our illustrious Governor Govinda Bandari on the Moon Griffon Memorial podcast. Thank you, Governor."

"It was my pleasure," Govinda says genuinely before hitting the end button on the screen of his in-dash interface. These interviews are a perfect way to spend a trip on the superhighway to Austin. Three months ago, at his inauguration speech, his message seemed to fall on deaf ears. Despite running and winning on a platform focused on bringing Louisiana back into the national conversation, he was faced with a disheartening lack of citizens willing to do anything. This was due in part to the fact there were not many constituents left in Louisiana to pander to. And they're not like the millions of immigrant families in the country, ready to start new businesses and make life happen. They're stubborn holdouts stuck in their ways. Again, he wonders if his parents made a mistake getting established in Louisiana, especially when no one else in his family thought this state would have more opportunity than inundated India. Though it could be the lack of competition in the realm of initiative is what has made him so successful. Bandari Casino would have never made it in Oklahoma or Las Vegas. This state can't ever seem to let go of its past, and even likes to replay it. If they don't respond to his dares, like the one he just left on the podcast, he may need to leave. He can't stomach staying at a table after it calls his bluff. He is still considering if it would be worth commuting from Texas to Louisiana daily when his car pulls in front of the Texas Governor's Mansion.

This is Govinda's third trip here. The old charm of the refurbished mansion leaves the Louisiana mansion, relocated to Natchitoches after the Mississippi river surge destroyed the original during Pilar, seem sparse and too modern. This white building speaks of a state which still has its sense of history, along with industry and people to move their economy forward. It doesn't hurt that the new financial capital of the nation is in Dallas now. Govinda is jealous. And Governor Guadalupe Martinez knows it.

"You like it?" Guadalupe asks Govinda from over his shoulder as he admires an old land survey map from the early nineteen hundred showing a much larger gulf coast. Her voice is both pleasant and smug. Govinda hates her.

"Of course I do."

"You can have it. I have some other ones I can frame. Bigger ones."

Govinda's round jaw flexes as he clenches his teeth. He turns, pulling his nose up as he'd been told by his house photographer in order to stretch out his double chin, and smiles tensely. "You are generous. But there are other things I'd like to see if you could be generous about."

"We've been over this, Govinda." Guadalupe moves over to her prominently displayed wooden desk and pours genuine whiskey into two glasses, the round, squat crystal decanter dwarfing her small hands. The decanter's shape mirrors Guadalupe's frame. Govinda palms the stout square glass, his shape very similar to this barware. He takes a large, impolite gulp to ready himself for what he must ask and the superiority he'll hear in the Texan's response, something all the water in the world can't seem to wash away from this state. Money is what he came for. But being in this building, thinking about his constituents stuck in a bygone era, gives him the notion there could be something more powerful than money. Just as calmly as he would set up his strategy on the flop in Texas Hold'em, he considers what is in his hand and changes his ask.

"We need a real capitol building."

"Govinda, you don't need a capitol. Nobody builds hundred-year buildings anymore. The only reason we have one is because of posterity."

"My state is turning into posterity."

"As is the rest of the world."

"Lupe, don't turn your back on us."

"You are stuck in the past. This isn't your grandfather's or even father's politics. With the Fed or corporations buying up all the land since we can't afford it, we're merely caretakers. We're the British Royal family, just with a little more color." She reaches a short finger out from her whiskey glass to touch his forearm, two shades darker than her own.

"You sit here and tell me this while your state has been able to keep its dignity. You haven't lost what we have."

"We lost Houston, Galveston, Corpus, Port A, Brownsville…would you like me to go on?"

"You didn't lose your identity," Govinda says, his voice rising slightly. He glares at her, his most recent eye surgery causing a red rim around his mud-colored irises. Early onset Macular Degeneration is worsened by stress and the nanotech he had implanted into his eyes has to work harder to correct his vision as it deteriorates. He doesn't flinch. He keeps his gaze and tone even despite playing at her table.

Guadalupe chuckles, "I can see why your casino customers elected you. But if you really want to talk about it, let's talk." Govinda takes a long draw of the whiskey to help overlook the insinuation that his previous career had something to do with his ascension to the governor's office. Guadalupe sits on her desk, and despite her small, squat stature, appears to get larger. "If you haven't been paying attention, our country is working from a $242 trillion deficit, for which your state is in the hole for more than most. Canada has a better GDP than us and soon will be as populated."

"Our state is in the hole for reasons beyond our control."

Guadalupe smiles and pours another glass of whiskey before leaning back on the desk while her pantsuit clad legs dangle childlike over the edge. "Let's assume for a second that's true. There are other states in line who need it more than you do."

"Are you talking about Florida?"

"Yes."

"We both know Florida is a lost cause. There is only one voting block left there. That money would be better spent on a state who could actually do something with it," Govinda declares with confidence surging into his voice. He's almost figured out her hand.

"Missouri, Nebraska, and Iowa could do a lot more with it. They are currently the freshwater suppliers of the country and could always use more infrastructure."

"We could be doing that!" Govinda squeaks out, though he knows what her rebuttal will be before he even finishes the sentence. He overplayed his hand.

"That ship sailed thirty years ago. And your state screwed us in the process. Had your predecessors capitalized on the federal funds instead of developing another corrupt state program in the Levee Department, especially when you already had a Levee Board, you would have been our fresh-water supplier and in turn been on the ground floor of an industry that has gotten bigger than oil. You passed and they capitalized. Kept themselves dry from those nasty seasonal storms in the process." She smiles and shakes her head before taking another big swig of whiskey. "Ocean right up the ass and you're still doing your grandfather's Louisiana personality politics."

He smirks this time since neither of their grandfathers were allowed near a governor's office. "We've all made mistakes," Govinda admits, trying to muster the same air of sober adulthood Guadalupe embodies, even as her small legs swing from her oversized wooden desk. He hopes this round is not over. "Not supporting each other was one of them. History gets written a lot faster these days since the changes can't stop. You sure you want to be known as the one who wouldn't help out your neighbor?"

"That depends," Guadalupe says matter-of-factly through a smile, "on if you want to be remembered as the state's second Indian governor with an over-inflated ego. Except your idea is to make a legacy in a dying state, squandering someone else's fading resources by recreating a giant phallus, one which will wash away in another twenty-five years."

The rest of their visit is short, cordial even. He's misjudged Texas and Guadalupe. He knows she's got her own constituency to worry about. If Texans weren't miserly business savages before, the climate has certainly evolved them into money beasts. When the New York Federal Reserve fell, and Dallas became the default financial center of the country, Govinda hoped keeping a good relationship with Louisiana's wealthy neighbor would keep them afloat. Maybe hope is outdated, something washed away with the world's biggest cities. But he's watched what symbols can do in his casinos, whether it be the calculated risk people see with playing cards, or the outright chance of the roulette wheel. Hope can drive a person to spend their last dime. They just need to believe it's worth it. Today he played his hand wrong, believing he could convince Guadalupe that a concrete capitol building in the shape of a middle finger, gesturing to climate change, is worth it. But the first rule of gambling is if you are going to bet against the house, you need to have something in your hand.

In his Mercedes he pulls out his dab pen and takes a long hard hit of the local brand. He feels his shoulders come down and thinks he might be able to sleep. Gone are the days of sleeping for exactly eight hours, waking with a sense of direction. After he took office, he quickly realized the stress of governing comes at a different price than the problem-solving in owning and managing. Convincing is not as easy as commanding. He reclines his seat into bed position.

While he procured this model two years before it became available to the public, he doesn't feel regret about the optics of indulging in advanced automation while his constituency hides behind levies using unsupported operating systems on aging service technology. Opening his latest casino while campaigning for governor earned him at least this. But now he second guesses purchasing this new nuclear line, with its line-of-sight shock-anticipating algorithms, only because the smoothness of the ride and quiet in the cabin makes it harder to sleep. He reminds himself the pockmarked roads of his state would not rock him but instead force him to put on a seat belt (something he has not used since he was a teenager). Rest is cut short by an incoming screen call from his assistant, another impediment to sleep he had not counted on. Constituencies don't wait until morning with their crises.

"Yeah," he says without looking at the screen or bothering to turn on the cabin lights.

"The depression is a tropical storm now. AI is saying it will get to Category 1 by the end of the night. It's building fast and following the same course as Pilar. The model put it at a Cat 5 by landfall. Maybe a Cat 6."

The number six causes Govinda to elevate his backrest and turn on his ring light. "How sure are they on the path?"

"Ninety-eight percent."

"Shit." If Louisiana takes another Cat 6 up the gut, it's likely to push the coast all the way to Alexandria, cutting away thousands of voter homes and some of his best customers at the casino. The governor's office was supposed to solidify his business and make the whole state his empire. An empire is nothing without people or land. These folks are liable to leave and not come back. And the ones that stay—and history dictates many will stay—will likely be exterminated by the storm. His mind races between dividends and floating bodies. If playing it safe has a higher likelihood of losing, Govinda has learned the correct tactic is to double down and hope no one sees through the bluff. *This is "the turn,"* he thinks. It's just the next round of this gamble. He can still work with this hand, but he needs to consider how to play the others at this table against each other. "Get a hovercraft prepped in Lafayette. I need a half dozen camera drones in the air, too."

The only organization, private or otherwise, which could come up with the required transportation in such a short time is the Cajun Navy. Govinda has never seen these people in his casinos, and he knows they didn't vote for him. He'd heard many here weren't happy with his proposed program to relocate them away from the coast. They didn't understand his "concerns" for their safety were campaign trail promises, and more of a concern for how much these mud rats cost the state by living here. Regardless, he marvels at their ingenuity and speculates he's overlooked a resource this state can still offer the world: its people. Specifically, the captain, one Errol Miller, seems to have an answer for everything, from hovercrafts on demand to Wildlife and Fisheries guides to show them the way. Once this storm passes, and he has made Louisiana matter again, he'll return to this place to see who's left of this rabble of sturdy citizens. They could be useful in garnering sympathy after the storm.

"Glad you thought of us," Captain Miller yells over the roar of the craft to the governor as he comes aboard.

"I have to take care of my state," Govinda attempts to say with his best campaign tone. Having to scream over the craft makes it sound more like a question.

Through the marshland and sparsely inhabited islands they travel, places where Govinda did not campaign in person. Neighbors and family crowd on the porches to glower as he goes by (though by the skeptical looks of some people on their porches twenty feet in the air he can tell they've seen his YouTube and Reddit ads). The guide, a young man of Honduran descent with a nearly shaved head and green coveralls, pilots the boat. They lose sight of land, and the hum of the hovercraft increases as they pick up speed.

Govinda sits on a bench, his assistant holding a waterproof blanket over the two of them so the sea spray does not ruin their suits. Once or twice, Govinda thinks he will be sick. He swallows enough to keep it in. The young guide glances at them and grins widely. The hum lowers as the craft slows, and Govinda emerges onto the outer deck to see the spire of the state capitol rising from a yellow brackish sea. They navigate between old warehouses and office buildings. When Pilar decimated the Mississippi River levees, they decided not to build them back. Eventually they are within feet of the forty-nine granite steps leading to the tower. Windows are busted out with evidence of sea birds finding their homes inside. The young Honduran man nimbly climbs the stairs and goes inside to check the nests. Govinda is nowhere near that committed to humans that run his casino. He stays on the steps in front of the capitol. His assistant gets the camera drones in the air though they struggle with constant 30-40mph gulf breeze. Govinda tries to get his remaining black hair to cover his scalp but eventually gives up. A lull in the breeze comes. He begins his speech.

"Here is Louisiana's past. What once was regal is now lonely and forgotten. As Hurricane Yara bears down on us we ask you: Are you ready for us to be gone? When New York was inundated we relocated money to Dallas. When San Francisco drowned we moved machines inland. Louisiana, the birthing canal of our great nation, is our soul. It is a feeling. It is a state of mind. It cannot disappear. But as you can see, if we don't give our soul a temple, it can be taken from us. This building stood as a symbol of hardworking, toughminded, men and women of yesteryear when life was better, easier. This building stood for our pride in them. We deserve to be proud again. Help Louisiana build a new state capitol. Click on the link below to donate."

The wind kicks back up and his assistant immediately begins editing the videos. The young Honduran clambers back on the boat, a clutch of eggs in his hands.

"That's a hell of job you got there," Govinda says to the young man.

The stocky guy, almost as stocky as Govinda, looks back with a wide smile. "Everyone and everything are doing their job." He carefully inserts the eggs into a portable incubator leaving Govinda to ponder what he was insinuating. His assistant appears next to him with a display of different camera angles. Govinda's hair looks like one of the birds' nests spilling from the capitol windows.

"We need to redo it. Can you swing us back around for another take?" he asks Captain Miller.

"No. The outer band of that hurricane is bearing down on us. Even if you could get your drones to sit still, we'd end up staying here too long and that storm will catch us. We have to leave now." The captain points to the bluish black tint of clouds pulsing with lightning.

"We'll get another break."

Captain Errol grins and pushes the throttle forward, pulling them away from the capitol.

"It just makes you look more desperate. Maybe that's a good thing," his assistant shouts over the din of the craft. Govinda allows him to send it to all the national news outlets.

It is early evening before Govinda is in his sparse capitol building. It has none of the grandeur of a limestone exterior, none of the opulence of Italian marble surrounded by orange and gold murals of topless mother figures plastered on the interior, as was in the previous capitol. The winds of Yara, perched in the gulf as a Category 6, reach Natchitoches. He can hear them through the gray concrete surrounding him. Onscreen the storm moves westward, the outer band pounding the little strip of land along Alabama's eastern border, the last habitable and solid bit of the Florida panhandle. He's already started the emergency processes by engaging the Coast Guard, the Navy, the Louisiana National Guard and requesting the Arkansas National Guard. He considers calling Texas but can't bring himself to do it. If Louisiana can make it through, they will need to shame Texas into helping rebuild. Patiently waiting for the touch up edits to his hair, he watches his squirrely young white assistant nervously take call after call. Eventually his assistant looks up from one of these calls with his hand to his phone chip implant in his ear.

"This is that captain from the hovercraft earlier; that Cajun Navy guy. He wants to know why you haven't sent boats down to his region yet?"

Govinda looks confusedly at him. "Boats?"

"Yes sir. We have around one hundred Rigid Hull Inflatable Boats in reserve the Louisiana Guard can use."

"No one told me we had boats. Get the Guard in them and get them to the coast. Make sure there are cameras streaming on all of them."

After relaying the message, the assistant remains silent for a while before looking back up at Govinda. "He misunderstood when he took you out in his hovercraft for…the…uh…media circus…that you'd…um…cut the bullshit for once. His words. All he wants now are boats so the Cajun Navy can do their job."

"You can tell him to kiss my ass. I'm not sending state government materials. They'll try and hock them for a quick buck after. I'm not an idiot."

In a much more diplomatic way, the assistant relays the message and the call is ended abruptly.

"What'd he say?"

"Let's just say he wasn't happy."

"You see what I have to work with? I took over a state of aging rejects and pirates. There was something that weird bird guy on the boat said. Maybe *my* job could be easier if Mother Nature would do *her* job and wash this all away."

"Sir, the calls keep coming in."

"And what do I tell them? That the worst hurricane since Pilar is going to kill them? Leave or die?"

"Um…Maybe something which instills a little more… hope."

The word is a slap to his face. Symbols of hope have been his agenda. Forward thinking took him too far into the future. A building in a faraway future, made much further by a cloud of destruction and uncertainty, can't help him or the people in his state right now. Anyone who survives this won't feel hope seeing an empty stone tower at the edge of the sea.

"Sir, the National Weather Service is reporting the coastal community of Britton Hill is gone." Govinda stares forward, his vision waning. Red rims his irises again, the nanotech trying to correct his sight. "Sir? The Florida panhandle is gone."

His vision fogs. *Gone. Like India*, he thinks. The monsoons which followed the epic drought, wiping the Indian subcontinent away, seem far away and long ago. But this is his country. He'd consoled himself that nothing of India was home to him since he'd never seen it. With a piece of America gone, he feels both losses simultaneously. Home is what he was looking for when he ran for this office. But Govinda knows floor plans and administration in casinos around the nation more than he knows the highways, the restaurants, and constituents of his own state. This is a real place, with real people. The problems they face aren't symbolic or economic. They're existential. Beginning to shake, he thinks of the faces on the porches as he cruised by in the hovercraft today. The faces haunt him. They are not chips to bet. What happens doesn't hinge on winning and losing. He can build a building, but it doesn't make it a home. How much would his legacy matter if it came at the cost of the only home he's known? What about at the cost of another's legacy? He will never be able to call another place home if he can't save this state from India's fate. Understanding washes into his mind. The link between identity and place is so tentative now. Land with no people, no legacy, is not a place. It's not a home. People with no land are still people. The fog in his eyes abates as the nanotech reclaims his focus. Govinda sees there can always be a second chance for a home, because home is just a thing that moves, just a symbol. Where we don't always get a second chance is with people.

"Call the Cajun Navy guy back. Tell him we'll send the boats. Get Guadalupe Martinez on the phone, too. And pull my car around. We're going to the coast."

Via the Mercedes screen Govinda sees Guadalupe behind her desk as if she does not have private chambers in which to sleep. "Please help, Lupe. I need your Guard. I need whatever influence you have in Salt Lake City to send electricians, solar generators, rescue drones, sat photos…anything."

"I'd be happy to. I see you're calling from your car. Should I make up a guest room in the mansion?"

"I'm heading south."

Guadalupe's round face drops and her voice becomes grave. "You don't need to prove anything. Dying with your state won't fix what's happening."

"No. It won't."

"Govinda, listen. What you're trying to do is noble and romantic. But that's not how everyone will remember this, remember you."

"That's all I've done in this office. I've thought about the future to figure out how they'll remember this. It isn't about me, shouldn't be about me. It's about these people. My people. I have to take care of my home."

Guadalupe smiles desperately, wishing she could speak reason, knowing it won't do anything. "Godspeed," is all she has left for him.

At nightfall on the marshy coast, Captain Erroll Miller is waiting for him. He stands on the deck of his hovercraft, a hand on his hip and the other holding his hat on his head against the wind. Being freshly shaved does nothing to hide the severity weathered into him.

"I just needed the boats. Your media circus will slow us down. Your drones can't fly in this." His gravelly voice is barely audible in the roar of the wind.

"No cameras," Govinda replies, removing his suit jacket and handing it to his assistant. He clambers onto the hovercraft awkwardly, nearly falling into the brackish water beyond the levee wall. "Just want to help some people."

"Understand something," Errol says with a deepening voice and a steady glare, "you get in the way, and I will move you. You're just a person like the rest of these folks."

"That's all I want," Govinda says. The size of his smile unnerves the captain.

Between the sea spray, the dark the craft's lights can't seem to penetrate, and the violent tipping of the boat, Govinda loses track of land. He turns to ask his assistant which direction they'd come from, only to remember he'd instructed him to stay ashore and keep up communication with the various departments. Seasickness finally takes over and he hangs over the side of the craft as they pull up to the first house. Miller smirks before stepping off the boat onto the third stair of the house. The water has already risen about four and a half feet. Returning to the boat with a family in tow, they sit away from Govinda, who retches like a freshman frat boy on a Saturday night. They eye him with even more suspicion than he'd seen from them earlier in the day. This is not how this is supposed to be. This is not how he wants to die. He wants to die as one of his people, leading them, not with them pitying him. Deep in the sloshing soup of his stomach, he finds a shred of resolve, enough to stifle the urge to upchuck just as they pull up to the next house.

"I'm going up on this one," Govinda says quickly to outrun the next heave.

Miller smirks again, an expression between condescension and knowing. "You have three minutes, then we move on."

Govinda hoped stepping onto something solid would stop the nausea, but it barely lessens it. Climbing stairs reaching into the heavens, the clouds are low and ominous. He arrives at a porch with an elderly man sitting in the dark, as if he'd been waiting for him.

"Poo yie but dis rain!" the old man says.

"We're here to bring you to safety, sir" Govinda huffs quickly. He can barely see the outline of the seated man. A dark rain jacket drapes over him and his chair. He can make out wheels on the chair. This man is elderly.

"I don't wanna go," the old gentleman mutters, voice barely heard over the rising wind. Govinda's eyes adjust more and he sees the old man is toothless.

"Sir, this house will be gone by morning."

"Den I will be gone wit it. I've had my time. I want to join my wife."

"Sir..." Govinda begins to reach for the wheelchair, not sure how he will manage it down two flights of stairs.

"Don't touch me you bastard! Dis is where I want to end! In my home!"

Govinda doesn't have time to reason more because the man has a quick convulsion akin to an unexpected, nasty burp, before his eyes roll and his head flops back. Govinda never bothered to learn CPR but he's sure the Cajun Navy will know what to do with this guy. He calls down to them over the side of the porch railing, but the roar of the wind overpowers his voice. Three minutes must be nearly spent. He grabs the man's arms and bends low, awkwardly putting the elder on his shoulder. He really should have put on an exosuit, but he did not think this is what helping would take. There are several moments when he believes he will drop the man or tumble down the stairs. Finally, he reaches the hovercraft, and with the help of Miller, lowers the old man to the deck.

"I always said Mr. Hebert would die before he'd leave his house," Miller chuckles over the wind.

"He's dead?"

"Oh yeah. Heart attack."

Govinda looks with the crew at the man he supposedly saved, now made a victim. The red rim around his irises are visible in the flashlights. The governor struggles to take everything in. It would have happened anyway, he tells himself, trying to stifle the shame rising in him like water on the old man's steps. The nanotech surges and he can make out the man's blotchy skin, his thin arms, and his toothless open maw. Even in lifelessness he looks as if he is calling to someone, maybe the wife he mentioned.

Ahead of the storm surge, Govinda receives his own tidal wave of actuality; his first real act of true leadership as governor is to kill a constituent. Whether or not he would have died is pointless. How he wanted to die is more important. He stands, contemplating for the first time if he is made for leading. His original plan for leadership was a simple, time-tested strategy. After stoking hope in his state, and discord with how the rest of the country treats it, his house would be too big to fail. He'd win pot after pot. But just like with Guadalupe and Texas, he overplayed his hand with this fellow and this storm. He bet wrong against a man's dignity. The bigger mistake was to play against a hurricane. It's impossible to be the house with weather like this. Climate is the house, and the house always wins.

"Looks like we're in the clear, though." Govinda meets the captain's eyes, hoping he means there is some forgiveness, some redemption, for his lethal leadership. "Just got word the storm is turning toward Texas. The freaky thing is breaking up." Govinda recommences to vomiting over the side.

THE GOVERNOR NEEDS TIME to sleep off the ordeal, as reported by his assistant to the press. Once he awakes, a press videoconference waits on several screens inside his bunker capitol building. All are curious about his decision to be at the front, helping his people with his own hands.

"You are focusing on the wrong things," he tells the press. "My story, our state's story, is one of crisis averted, but only temporarily. Louisiana's people are alive and safe, for now." He clears his throat before continuing. "We can't say the same for Florida. Louisiana may have felt the hot hand of Mother Nature rob from us, but Florida's panhandle has been taken completely. We mourn our Floridian cousins. We mourn our nation, having lost so much of itself to the sea." Silence consumes the crowd, and the reporters remain motionless in their screens. "Mother Nature has put us on the run. She hides the future from us, making us desperate dreamers in our attempts to survive. But with a future so uncertain, I choose not to forget how we came to be in this great nation. We became a force the world has reckoned with for nearly three hundred years. We have survived in the face of the impossible time and time again. Louisiana is not ready to forget that. In forgetting our history, we forget ourselves and make it harder to find a way forward." He pauses again, looking directly into his camera before continuing. "I want to erect a monument to Britton Hill, and to the lost Florida panhandle. It's true that in years to come this memorial, too, could be consumed by the water. But we are not upset the Jefferson Memorial is sitting at the bottom of the Potomac in D.C. Shame would have awaited us had we not built it. Florida's memorial, the memorial of a U.S. with fifty full states, can't be built by us alone. We need help from Texas. Call your senator and have them put pressure on our nation's financiers. We've lost so much. We will lose more. But *how* we lose is what defines us. See, we have a saying around here: 'If you don't act like it will stop, it never will.' Good afternoon."

The roar of questions begins as he mutes the conference app. His assistant approaches and directs him to video chat.

"Governor Martinez for you."

"Guadalupe," he greets her projected image with a pleasantly sober tone. Reporters continue to message him. Some wait in queue for interviews. His vision is crisp. He gives fatherly smiles to their images on the screens.

"You went from 'Florida is lost cause,' to putting me on the line to memorialize it. Nice angle," Governor Martinez says.

"Not an angle. I'm doing what's right by my people and by my nation. Even if I can't beat the house, I still intend to win a few hands." He smiles now. "Speaking of hands, do you need one? I know Yara is beating y'all up."

"You think you're cute? You're starting to sound like someone gunning for the oval office." Govinda responds with silence. Guadalupe's tone drops and she becomes grave. "Fine. I want to see the blueprints for this before I give you any money. I'm not letting you erect a Florida monument in the shape of your old state capitol."

He doesn't say anything at first, and she knows why by his face. A similar look appeared the night she visited his casino. He sets his eyes on her the same way he did on the river card as his dealer turned it.

Soaked

On the day his second crop of tomatoes dies, Catcher goes fishing. It is a perfect day for it: overcast and under one hundred. He pulls the bait up to his spot on the levee, thinking he'd had a bite, only to find it had caught on a weed. It's likely because the water, like the land, isn't supporting life like it used to. Catcher unscrews the reel from his pole. He snips the bait off so it won't swing around and hit him. Then he smashes the reel against the hard plastic dock. He snaps the pole over his knee. He gives both back to the water and stomps to his truck.

Before telling his truck to start, he levels his blue eyes on the flat, soggy corporate land before him. He turns his pug nose up at the acreage, the tip of his nose pointing to the gray sky. No one has farmed this land in a generation. Since the Gulf came up, and the rain came down, all the other families got out of the business. It is a business, after all, and taxpayers got tired of subsidizing the lost crops. He aches to continue with self-pollinating soybeans and sugarcane as generations had before him. But both struggle in the daily inundation. There is no way in hell he'll grow daikon radishes. No matter how much carbon it captures he cannot be complicit in sullying gumbo with the fake rice people make out of it. No one grows real rice because of the methane it produces. Makes no difference. He won't do rice because life is wet enough without his workplace being a paddy.

There aren't many nutrients in the ground anymore. And if water doesn't get what he grows, then the oversaturation of carbon dioxide in the air will make the food empty and flavorless. There was hope that tomatoes could put this water to use. They were his last chance. It was desperation which led him to plant in the winter months. It was stupid to reason the mild weather, never getting below sixty-five degrees, would make it work. And against his best judgement, Catcher spent all he had left of the savings, the retirement, and the seed money on nano-bees he'd never get to use. The tomatoes would never flower, and the little mechanical bugs would stay in their reclaimed beehive, a cute little marketing idea given there were no living bees left to populate it. This life is going the way of the bees; done in by water, bad air, and business.

He gets back out of the truck and shouts at the open land. There is no one to call mental health authorities. His son should be here, he thought. His grandson should be here too. No, they shouldn't, he chastens himself. He promised his wife in the months leading up to her death that he wouldn't push this life on them. It was his right to die working the land, but not their birthright. They didn't have it in them anyway. The strand of DNA that makes a man want to get up before dawn, work in dizzying heat, and age early, all to gamble on a plant's life, didn't make it to his progeny. He weeps.

The drizzle begins. "It was only a matter of time," he whispers. On a similar rainy day, his grandfather squinted into the sky and foretold this. He'd hoped he would not have to see the end of farming in his family during his lifetime. Scraping his boots against the running bars before re-entering his Ford, he sloshes through the mud towards home.

Designs on retiring died years ago when the crops began to fail. He knew he'd spend everything he'd saved trying to keep this up. He misjudged how fast it would happen. His world has been held together by the thinnest financial thread. There are scant social services in this part of the world. In a pinch, the Cajun Navy could keep him afloat. Any good feeling that may have visited a dyed-in-the-wool farmer upon the thought of accepting a handout are dashed when he sees his grandson's solar Toyota in the driveway.

"Today's not a good day, Quinlan," he announces as he opens the door. Quinlan bumps his head as he attempts to back out of the fridge. Even the sight of his pasty skin, skin unmarred by the elements, irritates Catcher.

"I had to go digging all the way in the back of your fridge for a beer, Pops. How old is this thing?" His lips curl as he stares at the corporate beer in his hand. Catcher grabs it from him and returns it to its place all the way at the back of fridge.

"This is an emergency beer. You only touch that on the worst day."

"So today wasn't that bad?" Quinlan's overly chipper tone sings the question.

Catcher belches, still staring at his grandson, daring him to be useful.

"I came by to tell you about an idea I had."

"Your ideas are shit. I can barely stand them when I'm in a good mood."

"But this one won't require money."

"Good. Because I'm officially out of it."

"Of what?"

"Money."

Quinlan's mouth drops and his eyebrows arch in shock. The brat really did think he'd hold on to some money for him. He must have mistaken the promise to keep him out of farming for a free down payment on his useless, productless life. The shock hanging on his face makes Catcher smile. He relaxes his narrow shoulders underneath the rain gear.

Returning his smile with accompanying brightness in his slate-colored eyes, Quinlan announces, "Well, now you are finally going to need me. Your land can be useful, again."

How he does it, Catcher wonders, is beyond what he can comprehend. Catcher will never be able to understand the post-Pilar generations and he doesn't want to. His bad mood reclaims him.

"My land is useful. To me. Now get out."

"Pops, come on!"

"Get out."

"I'll come back tomorrow."

He closes the door and locks it should the little cuss get high and decide to come tell him more of his dreams. He throws his blackened Caterpillar Deere baseball cap at the laundry room. He rubs his red eyes, scratches at his white stubble, and runs his fingers through his inexplicably dark brown hair until it is thoroughly messy.

"How am I the crazy one here?" he asks his quiet house. Only the dripping water outside answers. But that is the answer. Everyone else in his generation wanted convenience and connection. The consensus thinks he's crazy to want things like land. Being a privately-owned farm in Louisiana made his unfederalized/noncorporated land all the more important. As usual, the rest of the country looked at this as another backward-looking practice which spit in the face of safety and innovation. Everyone else says going corporate or federal is not only cost effective but the only way to ensure this most precious resource is handled with care. But Catcher knows Louisiana has been, and always will be, a place where hope is for the wild and living is for the strong.

When his wife's stage four diagnosis arrived, she couldn't understand why he wouldn't cash in for an urban life. Spending his days in a concrete cage—people sandwiching you from above and below, silence replaced by whirring and buzzing, views replaced by screens—would have been terminal for him. She needed his untamed strength to fight with her and for her. He resisted until her cancer-ridden voice stopped pleading for the city. He'd take her to the fields just so she could see things growing. Eventually, she thanked him. But his son, Silas, did not. When he stopped visiting, Catcher thought he'd purged the idea of spending life with fickle, listless city-folk from his house. He hadn't bet his grandson would be a bleeding heart—believing love could overcome the years of silence between Catcher and Silas without tempting the ugly side of either strength or wildness.

Catcher walks through the house, wondering what his grandfather would do on the day farming ended. Something needs to be done to make his grandfather proud. Something his grandfather would do. Appeasing the dead with ritual, especially on an occasion like this, always looks crazy to the rest of the living. But these most recent generations have changed away from the life that brought them here so that anything involving sense looks crazy. "If you act like it'll never stop, it won't," he says aloud. There's only one thing his grandfather would say needs to be done. He grabs his dingy hat from the laundry room floor and heads out the door.

IT RAINS THROUGH THE NIGHT. Catcher feels like he's going back in time with only rain as the constant. The drops get closer until he is wet. Opening his eyes to the same gray sky he saw yesterday, he watches the rain hit his face. It all went fuzzy when he got to the bar. The bartender, one of his oldest friends, said the look on his face was enough to pay for half his tab. Catcher took it as license to drink double. Several minutes of staring at a sodden sky pass before he decides to test reality by looking around. He's in his yard, in the same clothes from the night before. He'd survived the long drive home. Powering through what feels like an axe blade lodged in the back of his skull, he sits up. He touches his small head to check that it hasn't grown as big as it feels. There is no blood. Just a lump from where he drunkenly collapsed against the broken sidewalk leading up to his outdated wooden frame house. His truck's nose is buried in the ditch. At least he made it home.

Catcher dries, showers, and dries again. He exhales loudly at the thought of finding someone to get the truck out of the ditch. The thought is cut short. Someone is rummaging in his living room. Caught between knowing he should care about what he has left and feeling like he'd give it all away to a thief to be done with it, he tiptoes into his living room in only his bathrobe. The lack of warning from his monitor system should have been a clue. Quinlan is flipping through the financial records on his tablet.

"Holy shit, Pops! How are you going to live? What you have here doesn't seem like enough to get you through another year. Why aren't you getting the carbon subsidies? And how old is this interface?"

Catcher goes to his recliner and fires up the digital projector as Quinlan pulls up a receipt and plops onto the couch next to his grandfather.

"Ok, just listen. You've been right. This whole time. You were right about the solar panels. No one will pay for high-efficiency ones when the government provides them. You were right about me running for state senate on the platform of bringing Louisiana up to speed with South Dakota's tech farms. I won't say you were right about the fishing boat desalinators, though. I'd just need more money for the R&D and people could stay out on the water indefinitely." Catcher stares straight ahead at the weather report as if he'd see something new. "Look right here. Your receipt for the nano-bees. You have dumb ideas, too."

Now Catcher turns to stare. His own grandfather would have swatted him and been done with it. Catcher reminds himself things that make sense have no use in this time.

"You wouldn't understand," he grumbles.

"Of course, I understand. You just don't understand how much I understand. You love this place. You love what you do. You've spent your whole life trying to make this work. That's me. That's what I do, too."

"You don't do anything I do. You don't love any place. You're committed to nothing."

"It looks that way because I'm an idea guy. I grow ideas. And you could grow a crop that would set us both up."

"Shut up, Quinlan. I'm too hungover for this."

"Weed."

Catcher stares at the digital red blob symbolizing heavy precipitation moving away from his location on the screen. An aching head translates the word his grandson utters as the endless process of trying to keep invasive species from taking over, something reminiscent of his relationship with Quinlan. It takes him a moment to put together the word with the context. When he does his head hurts worse.

"I'm not your pot supplier."

"I don't need a supplier. I can get weed at any car charging station. What I need is better quality, same as everyone else. The corporate stuff is crap. Only the boutique growers make anything worth vaping. With the lack of regulations on potency in Louisiana we could make some good shit. We wouldn't have much competition. The seeds are in my car. I've already put in money."

"You know you're an idiot, right? You think buying seeds is the only thing that goes into farming?"

"No. It takes soil. It takes rain. It takes time. You have all those things."

"There's more to it than that. Which costs a lot more money."

"Dad said he'd pay for the upkeep of the equipment, the power supply, and pay you, until the first crop came in."

Catcher smirks at his grandson's naiveté. Quinlan looks at his father with the same grey, idealized eyes as he views Catcher. The big difference is that Catcher would be honest with him and wouldn't cover his second agenda.

"You're a fool head, boy. Your daddy hasn't ever looked out for anyone but himself. You didn't even ask him why he'd be willing to part with some funds for this particularly dumb idea of yours?"

"Don't have to. He's got cancer. Cannabis is the only thing that's helping. Said he wants to spend money on something that matters. Nothing to hide there because he doesn't have the energy or time it takes to keep up a lie." Catcher teeters between disbelief and grief. His son, Silas, had stooped to low lengths to try and get his father to move, to give him money, to treat his mother differently. But to fake cancer, and send his grandson with the news, the only family member his son knew he kept any tolerance for, would be too low. Catcher imagines Silas as the war of cancer wages in his body. Silas looks like his mother. A picture of the same long face, cut with sharp edges from the sickness, punches him deep in his gut. Catcher brings his gaze to meet Quinlan's. There's sadness there. Enough to make Catcher believe his son's illness is real. "He said if anyone could make this stuff thrive, it's you."

Had he not seen concern hanging in Quinlan's eyes only a moment before, he would have never believed his son would have said anything kind about what he does. There is too much happening for Catcher to get a good bead on it. The hangover and bump to the back of his head still feels like it's trying to cave his skull in. A flip in his stomach could be the tofu po-boy from the night before, backed by too much whiskey. He doesn't want to accept the thought of cancer—taking the only connection to his wife away from him. And then there is this twenty-four-year-old kid, yammering away about planting. The worst feeling, though, is what comes from thinking this could make sense.

"Let's take a ride out to your field and talk about what it would take. Wrecker should be here any minute to get your truck out of the ditch. You know, if you switch to weed you probably couldn't wreck a self-driving vehicle."

His grandson taking responsibility for something, not to mention something that helps him, nearly causes him to vomit. His truck back on four wheels, they begin their trek out to his wasteland. Catcher waits for Quinlan to mock his old electric model F-150—nearly an antique in comparison to Quinlan's solar model, and a dinosaur in comparison to the nuclear vehicles that rolled out this year—the same way the weather now mocks him by sending frightfully bright rays of sunlight, through normally perpetual cloud cover, to sear his bloodshot eyes. Fully expecting to disappear into silence while Quinlan yammers about this newest project, he is disappointed by the questions he's met with. They're innocent enough at first. On another day, with his bank account feeling bigger and his head feeling smaller, he might like the questions. They intrude into the overly personal.

"Why didn't you tell us you were going broke?"

"Because it's none of your business."

"It'll have to be my business now. Don't you—"

He's cut short by Catcher switching to self-drive and pressing the emergency brake as they pull onto the edge of his property. Instead of reviving his tomato plants, the heat of the naked sun steams the stalks and they deteriorate in their supporting cages. They are withered even more than they were the day before.

"What are those?"

Catcher ignores the question and walks through the rows. The ground squelches beneath his rubber boots. Quinlan stops after just a few steps, the mud already consuming his polyester canvas shoes. Catcher grimaces, watching the boy's plans wither with his tomatoes. Quinlan's soft middle pokes out as he exhales.

"Damn it!" The weed aficionado rubs his shoes on the running bars of Catcher's truck. "How many acres is this?"

"Just over two hundred."

"That should be about right."

Catcher's face drops. Even with wet earth working his way into Quinlan's shoes, he'll still have to explain this to his grandson.

"Well, what won't be about right is the water. The reason the plants are dying, the reason your shoes are ruined, the reason I'm broke, is it's all soaked. Everything you see. Even the Feds are starting to give up this land. This year could have the next hurricane that finishes it all off."

"That's all the time we need."

"You don't get it. This place is too wet. It's sinking. It'll kill anything you put in it." Catcher debates if all the pot and the other artificial knock offs Quinlan uses has made him stupid. He squints through the sun, the headache, and the stupidity, readying his thickest, most potent reality. Before the deluge of insults comes pouring out, he sees all the hope in his grandson's eyes. They look like Quinlan's father's eyes, Catcher's son, before the death of his mother made it to where they couldn't look at eat other. Quinlan's eyes even had a twinkle of Catcher's own youthful days. But a lot of hard life, filled with unforgiving decisions, has happened since then. Catcher can see the practical and the real, beyond the smoke and mirrors of dreams now floating in Quinlan's gaze. Catcher knows the reason he is the oldest private farmer in three states is because of his pragmatism, not because of his dreams. Life here must struggle. As days of plenty become a memory, and pragmatism replaced blind optimism for a life scratching out less than what is deserved, Catcher lost the resolve to crush hope. What might he have scratched out of life had he gotten out of the hope-crushing business a long time ago? One last look at this grandson's eyes, though, tells him destroying his dream would be a hard row to hoe.

Quinlan smiles at the eye contact. "The strain I have requires at least 550 gallons of water per plant. Dad got some averages from the Land Commission. Your land should be holding steady at about a hundred gallons per square foot. It'll still be wet for the plants. But I bet they'll make it. Plus, these plants are carbon sinks. We could get some government subsidies to add to the income."

Nausea attacks Catcher again. He doesn't like how much he's participating in this conversation. "Growing," he rebukes, "isn't just about water and air. There's pH to consider. There's not enough nitrogen in the ground. And I don't know if these cages I put out for the tomatoes could do anything for those plants in a storm. If they don't have strong roots an August thunderstorm will shred them."

Quinlan continues to try and clean mud from his shoes. Without looking up he says, "Dad said you'd figure it out. You always did." He gets frustrated with his shoes and looks up at Catcher. "Can't we just look it up?"

Against every instinct, Catcher agrees to sit in front of his dashboard touchscreen and look for more hope. Cannabis needs a soil pH around six. That's just about spot on for the clay underneath his topsoil, courtesy of the River. Then there is the matter of amendment and enrichment. Federal restrictions forbid the use of non-naturally occurring nitrogen. Trying to bring oxygen, and then life, back to the water in the delta means farmers can't use any of the cheap chemicals his grandfather used, the ones which made a dead zone now nearly the size of the entire Gulf. And as for wind protection, that's where this little endeavor falls flat. There is no structure cheap enough yet strong enough to hold against the wind. He'd have to rebuild the Superdome, only three times larger, to protect them. It'd have to be stronger than the Superdome, too, if a measly little Cat 5 blew the roof off back at the turn of the century. Catcher considers a non-structural approach. Bamboo can block wind easily. And it grows fast. Too fast it would seem. The whole crop would be overtaken in one season. He has no intention of spending every bit of his days wrestling with the spindly wood of one weed just to protect another.

"There's just too much to contend with. This gig is harder than anybody realizes. I'm sorry. I really am."

Quinlan stares out over the rotting tomatoes recognizing this would most likely be his crop's future. "This was Dad's idea, you know. I knew you didn't want any more of…whatever it is I do. He said the whole thing would be hinged on you. Because only you knew how to work earth when everyone else quit. Like you could bend Earth to your will, same as you did everything else. We're so close. Just a couple of logistics away."

"Logistics? Son, that's not logistics. That's nature. And you're dad's wrong. I didn't work shit. I got worked. Your grandfathers, your ancestors, worked harder and cut corners, doing things outside of nature, like amending the soil. We worked to build levees, but it keeps the fertile runoff of the rivers from renewing the soil. The Natives had it right. This land never belonged to us. And you can't work something that doesn't belong to you." He looks out the window in the direction of his house. His headache is getting worse. He can feel Quinlan staring at him. "The more you try to control this, the less you have control."

"Just say you'll think about it for another day. One day."

Hair of the dog helps the headache. It's easy to blame the bump on his head for his general unease. But the longer he thinks about that damn field, those goofy plants, and his forlorn grandson, he knows it's not physiological. His mind, honed by seasons, soil, and sun can't resist the puzzle of growing a crop. It's cruel. Just over twenty-four hours ago, he'd watched his family's legacy die. Now, witnessing its corpse in the coffin, he must listen to his grandson tell him it's still breathing. The smart thing would be to bury this, sell the land to the hungry Feds, and live out his days in this old, water-rotting house. It's only fair.

The hope in his grandson's eyes beckons him. Catcher wishes Quinlan felt that kind of hope looking at the soil and, instead of thinking of money, see how small he is. He'd wanted his son, too, to have hope like that when his eyes touched the family land. Being small, and then making anything magical happen anyway, is all one could hope for as far as Catcher is concerned. It is still hard for him to understand why this life was enough for everyone who came before but isn't enough for them. Empty promises of becoming someone caught his son. City fever took Silas, and nearly took his mother. His son still doesn't believe Catcher can't live that life. Just like Quinlan doesn't believe he won't be able to make this work. The earth isn't the same it was even twenty years ago. Every solution he comes up with is stymied by regulations, climate, or money; three things everyone in this state can't ever seem to get around. It was so much simpler when he was just worried about if he could get a second crop of soybeans out of the field, or how late in the fall he could harvest sugarcane. The past, arching up to this moment, brings the gift of an answer.

When Catcher isn't home the next morning, Quinlan tries his cell phone. The old man never answers, though, because he didn't bother getting the chip implant. Quinlan figures he's at his favorite bar. Logging into the streaming camera facing the parking lot he sees it is empty, and he gets worried. If the grumpy old goat wanted to off himself, he's finding extra ways to make Quinlan eat his spite. It wasn't supposed to happen like this. This was supposed to make them a family.

As he pulls up to the farm, the only other place he could be, the sight of drones moving back and forth allows him to exhale. But their work makes Quinlan cock his head in confusion as he gets down from the two-seater into the mud, feet remaining dry thanks to new vinyl boots. From the dash control panel, Catcher commands two airborne drone units to pull up tomato cages, another four units roll along to till and make rows, and another copter drone replaces the cages after planting a cannabis seed.

"You're tilling? Pop, that's releasing methane and carbon! No wonder you're not getting the carbon subsidy. You're poisoning everything."

Catcher doesn't look up from his panel, "Yeah, but I'm gonna grow your damn plants when no one else can."

"You are? Awesome! But you've picked the worst way."

"You want my help or not?"

Quinlan gets silent, reconciling morals and money. Certainly one little Louisiana farmer won't singlehandedly bring the planet to three degrees Celsius of warming. The added thought of losing his father's money along with his grandfather's budding respect decides it. After a time, he says, "Damn, these antiques are efficient."

"Even better in the summer when I can stay home in the air conditioning and run them."

"How long do you think this will take?"

"They'll need to charge tonight. But should be done tomorrow."

Quinlan surveys the drones. It looks like they remove and replace cages, till, and sow at a rate of about ten minutes per row. Quick math tells him it shouldn't take through tomorrow to do two hundred acres.

"Pops, why is—"

"The trick is your plants will need companions. It's an old Native technique. We are doing something similar to their Three Sisters. They would do squash, beans and corn. Beans fix nitrogen. Tomorrow these bots are going to plant soy around your plants. Can't believe I'm using it this way.

Fed's been trying to get me to use soy as a cover crop for years. Other thing we're worried about is wind. Corn used to help with that. In about two or three weeks, depending on how the sun treats us, we should be about ready to get some sugarcane in those rows between them and they'll be a windbreak like the corn would."

Quinlan walks until he is shoulder to shoulder with Catcher. The hum of the drones moves further toward the back of the property leaving silence and an open skyline for the two men.

"Dad was right."

Without a glance at Quinlan, Catcher starts his truck up and heads home.

Almost immediately Catcher regrets his decision to help Quinlan. After that day, the boy shows up twice, sometimes three times a week, talking about how to angle the product on the market, getting glassy-eyed just talking about the "quality." He wants to grow the business as if there is more land being made somewhere. Catcher listens until he can't anymore. Then he goes to take a nap. It's a better alternative than going off on the boy. Quinlan has no idea what this part of the work is like, either. He is terrible at waiting.

To avoid Quinlan, Catcher starts spending more time out on his land. He walks the rows the way he did with his grandfather. Exercise was sidelined during his father's era after he convinced his elder to invest in drones. As the days roll on, he goes further and further across his property. It all looks different since it's not on a digital screen. With all the other senses engaged, he stops feeling like he is watching his crop and instead is a part of it. He used to have favorite plants when he'd work with his grandfather. He notes seedlings in this crop which look different than the rest. He can't help looking over at this one cannabis plant whose purple hue is slightly darker than the others. He touches the plants feeling their cool leaves. If rain erodes some topsoil, he gently pats a little around the base, with his hands no less. He loses hours sometimes and stays into the night when he isn't satisfied that he'd checked all his favorite plants.

The lightness he finds in the field dulls somewhat when he watches Quinlan's car coming up the road one day. This patch of dirt had somehow become more sacred to him, and his grandson's company would spoil it. With only a raised head for acknowledgement, he goes back to tending his rows. Quinlan calls to him and Catcher merely waves over his shoulder without turning. Right afterwards, he hears the slosh of Quinlan's carbon fiber clogs and turns to see the boy walking across the top of a row.

"What the hell is wrong with you? You can't see where I left footprints? Walk where I walk!"

"Shit! Sorry! Sorry."

The young hippy entrepreneur smiles with excitement as he walks. "It looks great out here. They're really growing!"

"Getting them to come up isn't the hard part." Catcher descends back into silence and looks out over the land, taking a deep breath, willing the moist earthy air to plant him solidly again.

"Can I do anything to help?" Quinlan's voice is an abomination; the greedy excitement cutting through the natural peace.

"You can hush."

Silence returns to the point where he can hear the wind rustling pines a quarter mile away.

"Why do you do that?" Quinlan asks, perverting the silence.

"Do what?"

"Why do you always shut people down?"

This is what Catcher avoids. This was why he and his son couldn't get along. No matter if what he does is working, for him, or for everybody else, he has to justify it and is expected to change. He gently toes a three-inch-tall soybean sprout.

"You see this plant. If you give it what it needs, and not too much of what it doesn't, it'll thrive. It'll provide for you. Every single time. And it does its best work when it's left alone."

From the confused look on the stoner's face he can tell Quinlan doesn't get it. But it does shut him up. Quinlan looks from sprout to sprout, trying to figure it out. Catcher's not sure, but he can almost see a farmer's twinkle in the boy's eye. Quinlan follows him as he slowly walks the field, checking each sprout. Catcher hears the air again. Nearly an hour passes before either of them say anything.

"This is what farming used to be." It's Catcher who speaks first.

"Why'd it change?"

"Depends on who you ask."

"What do you think happened?"

"We forgot how small we are. These plants know. They are prepared for the day-to-day battles. It makes them adapt. When you lose those little battles, over and over, you learn what's important. You know your place. And if you're not in your place, you move toward it. Stop losing the little ones, you end up thinking you're big, and lose the big battles because of it."

Quinlan is quiet for a second, taking in the philosophy of his elder. There's only one thing to make this old-world knowledge make more sense. "Let's go get high."

"Is that all you think about?" Catcher growls at him.

"Farming is all you think about. I'm trying to meet you halfway. Might as well get you better acquainted with what you're growing here."

Quinlan shouldn't be surprised his grandfather has never smoked, but it's difficult to wrap his brain around someone not buying something at a charging station or a bar. There's more dispense depots now than there are synthetic coffee shops. Quinlan blinks through the vape haze beginning to form in his grandfather's living room, appreciating how weed has become so ubiquitous since syn coffee and alcohol are more expensive. He looks over at his grandfather and sees him staring wide-eyed at the wall. The geezer looks so freaked out that Quinlan checks the cartridge in his dab pen to make sure he did put in Tripping Travis brand.

"Pops. You ok? Pops!"

"It makes me hear you funny. Like you're underwater."

"Yeah. That's supposed to be a good thing. I think you're broken."

"It's weird."

"Lean into it."

Catcher's eyes don't leave the wall. As the sun outside sets, silence and dark seep into the house. His eyes draw down. He tries to get used to the humming quality his thoughts have taken. But that internal humming is distracting. After several minutes, Quinlan decides to try the conversation with his grandfather again.

"What'd you mean about plants thriving when you leave them alone?"

"Doesn't seem like a hard concept," Catcher answers in a near whisper, the growl of his frustration noticeably absent as he tries to figure out the watery hum.

"Is that why you wanted to farm? So you could be left alone?" Catcher blinks drowsily but doesn't answer. "Because I think you're wrong." Catcher turns to him, sternness peeking through his slack expression. "About the plants thriving and being alone."

This talk about his life and what he wanted, against the liquidity of his brain, is ruining whatever positive effect this weed had. "You are stupid," he tells Quinlan.

"No. No. I'm not. You said it yourself. Lose the little battles because it will make you move to your place. Your crops have been dying until this year. You've been losing a lot of crop battles. Lately you've stayed out there with them.

They're thriving because you changed something. They're thriving because you're in it with them, not because you left them alone."

"You know how stupid you sound?"

"About as stupid as a high grandfather arguing with his high grandson."

Catcher looks back at the wall lazily. "We'll see."

"TIME TO GET UP. WE GOT CANE TO PLANT." The slack expression is gone from Catcher's face. His Caterpillar Deere cap is already on his head and his rain gear is on.

"I thought we could do that from your couch on an interface."

"I never said that. Besides, it's not the same. Get your shoes on."

Quinlan is angry when he walks outside and sees the sun still isn't up. He cinches the hood on his recycled cotton pullover to fight the damp. The last time he'd been awake this early was because he hadn't gone to sleep yet. He says nothing as his grandfather touches the navigation panel, bringing a blue glow to the cabin. The dim light makes angles in places where they usually aren't. In this light, Catcher looks like a giddy child. Quinlan sees his grandfather shaved, and his stained cap has been replaced by a crisp new one.

A large truck full of short brown stalks is parked on his property. Catcher exits and greets the driver with more friendliness than he has ever greeted Quinlan. The sound of excitement makes Quinlan sink further into resentment at the rude wake-up. The truck driver drops his load on the edge of the property and Catcher touches the screen in the truck, sending the drones to work. Quinlan watches the red and white flashes of the drones as they flit back and forth from the pile of cane stalks to the field.

"Just got to watch the moon. The moon will tell you how the water is moving in the ground, like the tides. My guess is the soy will get mature in about four weeks. So about three-quarter waning moon." Quinlan continues to sulk, wondering why this is more interesting to the curmudgeon than Cannabis strands. "Not too many people go by the moon anymore. But it's rarely ever wrong. I've been pulling plants and had Fed farmers stopping by to laugh. Two weeks later, when their computers told them it was time to harvest, their plants were sitting drowned in the fields. So many things in nature will tell you what you need to know, put you back in your proper place." The sun breaks over the horizon, winking at them from underneath low clouds. "Let's get syn coffee. We'll come back and check on the drones."

Quinlan's mood improves with syn coffee, but bad news is waiting for them when they return to the field. Several of the drones returned to their chargers despite having nearly full batteries. A couple remain on the task of planting sugar cane and covering them with mud. But several more are deconstructing the rows where the first sugar cane was planted. Dirt covered stalks lay strewn between cannabis and soy. Swearing, Catcher shuts down command operations, sending all drones back to the charge dock.

"Come on," he growls at Quinlan.

"Where?"

"We need to replant those cane!"

"Yeah. And your drones will do it."

"That operating system is twenty years old and unsupported. It hasn't been updated since you were a kid. It glitches. A lot. Then it takes about four hours to reboot. We're going to lose the cane if we don't get them up out of the wet mud and onto the rows. We gotta get them all in the ground."

"Pops, four hours isn't going to matter."

"You want this fucking crop or not?" he shouts. Quinlan knows his grandfather's anger, but not his rage. This may be what his dad was talking about, the reason he left. Not wanting to find out more he exits the truck. In the back there are medieval looking tools. His grandfather calls them a shovel and a hoe. Quinlan stifles his chuckle at the second name and shoulders it. Luckily, he remembered to wear the vinyl shoes because the rows are still sopping wet from rain the night before. After Catcher reforms the row with his shovel, he teaches Quinlan how to make a furrow, drop cane in, and pull dirt on top with his hoe. They move about fifteen feet when the annoying mist becomes an unforgiving downpour. Quinlan groans from underneath his cotton pullover.

"Ok. Time to go." Quinlan shouts over the hiss of the rain.

"No. Opposite. Work faster."

"I can't work faster!"

"We'll lose our money and our planting time. You can't count on a second chance here."

Catcher's shovel begins to work again, slapping together the rows more artfully than any machine could. Quinlan tries to keep up. The truck is just fifty yards away. He could leave this maniac here. But looking at his grandfather, soaked, and smiling beneath the lowered brim of his new hat, makes it hard to walk away. If he leaves this old man to tend his investment, he'll never be able to come back. The wild look in Catcher's eye and his distaste for weed could lead him to do something desperate. He tries to think about what makes him small and what his place is right now. Something tells him this is his chance to show him he's really Catcher's grandson. He moves his hoe faster. The strokes start out sloppy with the fast pace but quickly become efficient and clean. So efficient, in fact, he doesn't look up to see how far he's moved until Catcher's shoes are nearly in his strokes. They get to the end of the row and the rain still pours. Without much of an upward glance they start to work on the next row. Grandfather and grandson fall into a rhythm. The *skif, slap, flerch,* and *guff* of their tools make a song in Quinlan's ears. He gives words to it.

"My weeeedddd is a-growin', these stalks are a-showin', while the rain is a-po'in, in Lousiannnnnin'."

Catcher looks over his shoulder with a smile without breaking the rhythm of his shovel strokes. "Don't you daaaar-reee miss stroke, or these stalks'll be soaked, then you'll looooooossssssse that big toke, in Lousiannnnnin'," booms out from him, his growl replaced with baritone.

Both men laugh as they work. The rain abates as they finish what was undone by the drones. They smile and pant. The drone dock blinks back to life, fully rebooted. The little machines pick back up on the row next to them. Quinlan rests his arm on his upturned hoe and laughs harder.

"You're going to be sore tomorrow," Catcher tells him.

"Worth it," Quinlan pants back.

QUINLAN NOW COMES BY THE field every other day. He won't say much as they walk the rows. Catcher does most of the talking. He talks about Quinlan's great grandfathers and what the land was like back then. Catcher details how change happened slowly in his youth and then faster when he was an adult. Quinlan wants to press him on if this was a function of age or climate but decides against it. The walking, the work, and the words are really all he needs. He sees no reason to interrupt the erosion of the old man's quiet built up over the years. Nights are different. Retreating to his grandfather's sagging house, never remodeled with modern water-resistant building materials, he becomes gregarious from marijuana. His grandfather returns to his silence, offering back only sleepy stares or muffled laughs. One night, though, Catcher's quiet is sullener. He says little and goes to bed early. Quinlan decides to follow him into the fields the next day. When they pull up in the early morning grey and rain, Catcher sits in silence, staring at his field for a while. He taps the touchscreen and sets tilling drones to work. He never exits the truck. Quinlan doesn't either. Both watch as the drones roll along, tilling the hearty soybeans into the soil around the cannabis.

"Seems wrong," Catcher finally says.

"Just remember it's part of the plan."

"Plan." Catcher rolls down his window and spits, not seeming to mind the rain coming into the truck. As if he still wasn't rid of the word, he scratches harshly at his regrown white stubble and at his belly, which has shrunk from all the row walking. "People and plans. Ain't a single goddamned plan what works out in the end. Time eats plans, shits out reality."

"I need to stop wasting my good stock on you. Why are you in such a bad mood this morning?"

"For the first time in five years, I had a viable crop of soybeans *and* sugarcane. I'm pushing half of it into the dirt. Ask me if I planned this."

"What are you worried about? You'll make quadruple what you would have in soy and sugar off this."

"It's crap. You can't even eat it."

"Yes you can. You can do a lot of things with it. What happened since yesterday?"

"This isn't farming!"

"Who gives a shit? It's what will make us survive! Fuck! You're more stubborn than Dad let on."

The truck cabin, charged with the volume of their voices, feels like a powder keg in sudden silence. Both men stare ahead, not daring to glance at one another. Quinlan fears to meet his grandfather's blue eyes and the finality of rejection there. Catcher doesn't want to let rage turn him into the monster his son told him he was the day he left. He reaches over and taps the touchscreen. The drones retreat to the dock. Then he touches "HOME" on the drive panel.

Throughout his youth, Quinlan struggled to find the value in the silence held between his father and grandfather. He rebuked his father constantly on his lack of communication.

He deigned to understand his grandfather's poverty of speech. Now he truly understands. The space kept by silence made sure that all involved were not threatened by the truth. What had seemed like a completely dysfunctional family now looks like a perfectly constructed apparatus, run and held together by silence. To pay homage to his newfound wisdom, he removes any further possibility of inconvenient truth from their relationship by staying away. This lasts for almost six months. By that time Quinlan's optimism has burned through his better sense and he decides to make peace. It'll have to wait until morning, though. One of this state's legendary angry August thunderstorms blows through. The kind where the rain comes in sideways and thunder shakes the ground like an earthquake. By dawn the wind is still vengefully blowing. Something from the back of his mind gnaws at him, something bigger than the annoyance of not being able to go out when he wants to. Then he remembers what the sugarcane was for.

A balmy afternoon emerges when the storm stops. He doesn't bother to call his grandfather. Quinlan drives out to the field where he's sure Catcher will be. He hopes Catcher will be walking through his rows, lovingly running his fingers across the tops of lush cannabis. Quinlan hopes there is still a crop there after last night's storm. But then again, it would not be surprising if Catcher tilled the cannabis into the soil instead of soy. This thought does not sadden him. Instead, fear that his grandfather won't be at the field, having given up the way Silas gave up on Catcher, fills his mind. The old man may have even flattened everything in a fit of heartbreak. The image wets Quinlan's eyes. When he arrives, he is confused to see neither has happened.

Walking past Catcher's truck, he looks down each row for his grandfather. On every row the soy is gone, tilled long enough ago that the ground has been beaten flat by his grandfather's footsteps. The cannabis must be eight feet tall, the cane twelve. Both put off strong odors, which, when combined, make Quinlan think this is what Eden must've smelled like. He reaches to touch six-inch-long buds on the cannabis, but is drawn instead to the fibrous, sturdy, green stalks of the cane. They must be almost three inches in diameter.

"Crazy, ain't it?" Quinlan turns to his grandfather who stands freshly shaven and smiling, leaning on his hoe, about four feet away. "Normally takes nearly a year for cane to get this big. Storm didn't seem to have messed with either of them. Not a single plant down. Those were sixty mile an hour winds last night. You should see your face right now, though. You look worried like a farmer."

"Yeah," is all Quinlan manages to get out.

"I was waiting for you try it out." Catcher reaches and breaks off a bud from a very purple plant. "Had to go search-ing online for when the best harvesting time is since you haven't been around. Turns out it's right about now. Didn't know you could do all kinds of stuff with these plants, like eat it. Anyway, I've been watching this one since he was just a little thing. Seems to be the best of the bunch." Quinlan brought it to his nose. It has the skunky smell he expects, but it has taken on the sweet of the cane growing around it and the richness of the soybeans at its roots. "I think tomorrow will be the day."

That night Quinlan is formally introduced Catcher to a cannabis press for vape oil. He'd always wanted one, heard it really was the only way to enjoy it fresh, but never thought of getting one. The idea of handling live plants, and the likelihood that he'd ruin the bud, put him off. Here is his grandfather, using drones with old operating systems and still self-driving his truck, getting comfortable with tech— bridging this gap for him. The press is a new ritual Quinlan very much likes. One bud produces only a drop or two of oil. But that was plenty for what they needed. After each have a decent pull, the oil is spent.

Quinlan instantly weighs one thousand pounds. Where most modern strands either turn your thinking up, relax you, or make everything funny, this does all of that, and none of it. It is as if he's existed incorrectly up until this moment. Quinlan sees himself staying here forever, letting this penetrate every part of his existence. Looking at Catcher, whose eyes are not wide or not shuttered, he could tell the farmer feels it too.

"This is good," Catcher says. "This is really good."

"This is better than good. You high?"

"High? I'm soaked."

"Soaked?"

"Yeah. First time we did this, it was like just my ears got high. Heard you through water. Now…I am the water."

"I think you just found the name. Pops, you have created Soak."

"*We* created Soak."

Quinlan's narrow eyes meet his grandfather's blue ones. There is no malice there. He thinks at first it must be this potent stuff making him lovey, but what he sees in grandfather's eyes has not been manufactured. "Why'd you go through with it?" Quinlan asks. "When you sent the drones back to the dock, I figured you were done with this."

"I was. Then I came home to this lonely hell hole. Kept thinking about tilling perfectly good plants into the ground. How I was ruining my last good shot. I had to think about what gave me that shot. It was you and this wonderful shit we're smoking. Those beans, the cane, they wouldn't have survived by themselves. This needed a companion in the crop and a new way of doing things. I had to take a piece of the past and the present to make it happen. Putting those beans in the dirt was like giving them back to my grandfather. I didn't need them anymore. With the way this place has changed, I realized it would take all we have; past, present, technology, and old farm tricks. You were right about all of it. I hadn't been small enough." From deep within the Zen-like essence he inhabits, Quinlan feels his soul bloom. "You and your dad. You were both right."

Before dawn, they set the drones to work and they dress. A pile of cane waits for them when they arrive at the field. Trucks arrive. The pile of cane shrinks while drones continue to pluck and pack buds. The harvest takes twice as long as expected because the trucks need to make two loads. One caravan of trucks takes the buds, another takes the cane. The sun shines mid-afternoon, burning off the mist. Naked cannabis plants remain, lonely without the cane.

"Till them," Quinlan says.

"You sure?" Catcher asks with some amusement. "I saw we could 're-veg' them, try to save them for next year."

"We don't know what that would do to the bud quality. Besides, half the fun is the growing."

Catcher smiles and touches off the drones. It is dusk on the second day before everything is done. They watch in comfortable silence as the last drone resettles into the dock. Both men look at the field. Only the rows are left. Quinlan sees something in the fertile emptiness. Just yesterday this place was filled with life. Now it's just potential. Next year might not go like this. There are no givens in this place. Inside how scary that is, beneath how ambiguous it leaves any semblance of surviving, it makes him feel small and very alive. So much more alive than he feels when he vapes. He and his grandfather are even more alike than he thought. They return to Catcher's home where both have another long, quiet sampling of Soak. Contentedly they retreat to bed early. Buyers will have their sum in the morning to tell them just how rich they will be.

Green glows behind Quinlan's eyelids. His access watch blinks with a secure message from the cannabis buyer. The offer is triple what he thought it would be. Attached is a no-compete retainer contract, forbidding Quinlan and Catcher from selling to anyone else for a generous monthly sum. Quinlan screams. He dances. He cries. They did it. Catcher is remarkably quiet through this. Quinlan figures he may have gotten into some of his hidden alcohol after he went to bed. He goes to Catcher's room to rouse him. Catcher's lips are blue, a deeper blue than his eyes.

The buyer sends emails every day leading up to the funeral. Quinlan brushes the green flashes aside. He must plan everything since his father's cancer worsened and his mother is staying with him at the hospital. Despite his disorganized financial records, Catcher had his will in an easy to find place: an old USB stick taped to the back of the fridge near where he'd hide his emergency beer. He said he reserved it for the worst day. Quinlan cries when he recognizes his grandfather believed it would have been the worst day for his son and grandson, but not for him. What Catcher did not know when he put his emergency beer back there is that it would not be the worst because he saddled them with his farm's debt. Quinlan downs the beer in one gulp, tears and beer running down the side of his face, wishing he was drinking with his grandfather in celebration.

The service is small. His ashes are put in a plant canister, ready to grow a tree, or maybe sugarcane. Quinlan goes to his grandfather's favorite bar after the service. It's a long drive. Seems appropriate that it's named "The End of The World Bar." There are several people chatting over beers. Laughter and music cut through the dreariness of the drizzle, heavy as mourning. An impressively chipper bartender pours him a spiked yerba mate.

"You must be Catcher's boy."

"Yeah. How'd you know?"

"You look tentative like him."

"Good to know I can do it in his place."

"What do you mean?"

"His funeral was today."

"Shit," the bartender, Chuck, says with genuine sadness. "I'm so sorry, my man. Catcher was…he was one of my favorites. I mean that. You're on the house all day."

"Thanks. I shouldn't be too expensive. Was never much of a drinker. Now I don't know if I'll be much of a smoker."

Chuck waves off a request from his employee. "Figure it out, Rosco." Turning back, he asks, "What's your name?"

"Quinlan."

"He'd talk about you. Told me all about y'all's plan to grow weed. Just about twisted him in two to grow something other than what he knew. But you made him a believer. He said you knew what you were doing. God, I still can't believe he died."

Quinlan takes a long gulp of spiked yerba mate to fight the tears back. He's tired of crying today. He clears his throat to get rid of remaining, stubborn sobs. "Yeah. He's dead. And I knew what I was doing. Problem is—I didn't know what *he* was doing. I didn't pay enough attention."

"I don't follow."

"We made the best bud the world has probably ever seen. But it was his farming that made it happen. While we put him in the ground today, I thought about trying to do the next season without him. Then I realized: I don't know when to plant the cane according to the moon. I can't tell you when to till the soy in the ground. I don't know how to adjust the stupid, delicate pH in this soil and moisture composition. He just knew those things intuitively. You can't look that shit up online because the weather and climate change all the time."

"No. No it isn't. Catcher kept it all in his head. That's why he was one of the last real farmers." Chuck watches as Quinlan loses the battle against his tears. "But, you're rich, right?"

"Last I looked it was enough to cover my father's investment costs, give him some cushion while he goes through the next round of harsh treatments. If I calculated right, it seemed like there would be enough to give us seed money to grow this strain even further. Maybe rent more land from the Feds to build bigger crops. But I don't know how that will happen now."

"You say last you looked?"

"Yeah. I've gotten several more messages from them. They've probably pulled the contract by now, given how bad this has gone." Quinlan flicks his watch and projects the most recent message onto the wall. The message is full of panic, as well as commas and zeros. They both stare at the sixty million payout.

"It turns out I'm rich," Quinlan says amusedly.

Chuck looks up and scratches at his thin throat. "This is pretty terrible of me, pretty crazy even, to ask if you'd be looking to invest."

"Well, my Pops did say you were good at crazy."

"This bar does ok. If it did weed, maybe even syn coffee, it'd do even better. A guy could take something like that anywhere. It could even compete in Colorado."

"Yeah. Yeah it might." Quinlan downs the drink. His tan hand pushes the glass over to Chuck with an expectant look. "Another of those and I'll go give it some thought."

"You're gonna go think it over at his land, aren't you? Like he would."

"That's not all that land is good for."

"You're thinking of selling it to the Feds?"

"Nope. I go there to Soak and feel small."

Acknowledgments

The land this book is centered upon is the ancestral home of the Choctaw, Houma, Atakapa, Chitimacha, and Coushatta. But that land is disappearing. Already, the Isle de Jean Charles Band is having to relocate due to the rising sea. May they find a new place that feels like home, in hopes we can do the same should the time come.

There is so much gratitude to share with so many people who made this book what it is. Thank you to Cornerstone Press for making *Soaked* part of The Legacy Series. Dr. Ross Tangedal and Eva Nielsen are visionary editors. And thank you to Ava Willett and Sophie McPherson for bringing this book to where readers can find it. Erin Bass at *Deep South Magazine* published a previous version of "The End of the World Bar," on 8/30/2018, sparking the idea to write more stories in this world. She, and the magazine, have been incredibly supportive. Kristi Guillory Munzing was kind enough to let me use lyrics from "Faut tu Voir" (album: *Light the Stars*, Valcour Records) and lament with me about not having easier francophone options for drafting emails. Gretta Gardner and Keston Bernard Lyons shared wisdom and experience with me to make characters alive and respectful. Amy Tao Foster not only lent me a most treasured name, but she taught me who a character was supposed to be. Dr. Maria Timm and Dr. Pamela Moore were the best beta readers. David Cartwright continues to be my literary teacher and cheerleader.

To my family I give the greatest gratitude. Not only do they allow me time to chase these ghosts inside my head, but they serve as the greatest inspiration. Watching my kids play allows me into their world long enough to find new stories in mine. And of course, there is always Emily. She is a story I never tire of.

Toby LeBlanc is the author of *Dark Roux* (2022). His writing has appeared in *Barrelhouse Magazine, Deep South Magazine, The Writing District,* and *Coffin Bell Journal,* among others. He was born in Southern Louisiana and currently lives in Austin, Texas.